A Machine for Hugs

Galen Gower

Sloth & Envy Press

Cover art & illustrations by Jason Tetreault

Sloth & Envy Press – Visit our website https://slothandenvy.com

Sloth & Envy Press logo courtesy of Fran McKinney

ISBN: 979-8-9923631-2-8

eBook ISBN: 979-8-9923631-3-5

For Caroline, with all my love

Contents

The House Under the Oak Tree

P aul needed to dig a hole to bury his hamster, Chubbles. None of his pets had ever died before, but now that he understood what it was, he realized his Grandma would die. Mom and Dad would die. He would die one day, and there was no escaping his fate, not now that he knew what *dead* was. He didn't understand and no one could explain to him why they all had to die.

When he put the shovel in the dirt the first time, it struck concrete. He uncovered a step, and then another. By lunchtime, Paul had uncovered a whole set of tunneling steps leading down to a perfect double of his house underground. He stepped through the side door and wiped his feet on the mat out of habit. The kitchen was gloomy with no light coming in the big picture window by the table in the nook. Down here in the house under the oak tree, his dead parents sat at the kitchen table.

Do you want a sandwich, Paul? Maybe an egg salad, Dead Mom said, though she didn't get up from her place at the table. She hadn't gotten up to clean the dirt off the windowsills, or vacuum the piles of dust off the carpet, or to do anything else, either. Dead Mom stared at the wall with her sullen and dry face tilted upward slightly, like she had just asked an angry question.

Lunch sounds great, doesn't it Paul? I'd love to stick around, but I've got to get down to the office for a meeting with important clients. Not all of us get the summer off, you know, Dead Dad said, but he didn't toss his car keys up and down to show he was in a hurry. Dead Dad didn't stop for a drink after work or make dirty jokes when it was just the guys in the shop. Dead Dad always made time to watch Paul practice his newest magic tricks, but he'd have to show them here, in the kitchen.

Dead Mom and Dad never moved. They sat at the table with their empty coffee cups, desiccated and shriveled, where they'd be dead forever.

"Don't worry about me, guys, I'm not going to stick around," Paul said. A centipede wriggled out from under the quarter-round where the wall met the floor. The whole house shivered with the clicking and scrabbling of tiny legs feeling for small openings between every joint and crevice.

Paul flipped on the lights in the family room. The stench of rotten mud overwhelmed the other smells, but mildew, mold, and rot drifted through. The couch was the same as his, but the cushions were discolored with dark stains where his parents usually sat to watch the news.

Paul glanced out the window but could only see the puzzled track of blind worms' tunneling and the grasping roots of the big oak tree in his backyard, up above.

"I bet the television doesn't get very good reception down here," Paul said and made his way down the hall. It was dark and he held his breath and tried not to make a sound. He did the same thing when he had to pee in the night and didn't want to alert anything else in the house that he was awake.

Down here, pictures he didn't recognize hung in frames on the walls in the hallway. He looked the first one over and trailed a finger across the top of the frame. Paul pushed a small pile of dust to the edge of the frame, and then over. It drifted to the floor, falling straight down, the shortest route to the carpet below.

There was a picture of smiling Grandpa Irving. A gold-framed photo of his Uncle Carl. A Kindergarten graduation scene of a girl he didn't recognize.

"All of you are dead down here, aren't you?" Paul squinted at a faded snapshot of a dog and a cat. He remembered a dog with crooked tail, but not the cat in the picture. "I never had a cat!"

Paul fled and didn't look at any more of the countless frames hanging on the walls. Only the dust swirling in the hallway behind him showed he'd ever been there. Nothing else stirred the air as he reached the doorway of his bedroom. Except this one belonged to Dead Paul, of course.

You want to see my baseball cards? Dead Paul asked from the bed. He didn't get up to get them down from the closet, or offer Paul a place to sit on the narrow twin bed. He didn't ask Paul if they had the same outer space-themed bedspread; he just lay there with his mouth open and didn't breathe or cough or laugh.

"I have the whole set of 1978 Fleer Major League Baseball, but my favorite is Rolly Fingers," Paul said.

Dead Paul didn't look impressed, he just lay there, taking up the whole bed. You didn't have to be alive to be considerate; Paul didn't have anywhere to sit. The sturdy toy box lid might have sufficed, but Dead Paul didn't keep his room any neater than Paul's and his dirty clothes and mud-crusted sneakers were piled up there. Mold spread from the ceiling to the floor along one wall and spoiled the look of the comets and ringed planets on the wallpaper. With nowhere to sit and nothing better to do, Paul reached up on the closet shelf and pulled down the shoebox full of baseball cards. The box was slimy on the bottom and the cards stank of mildew, but Paul sat on the floor to see if Dead Paul had any of the cards he was missing from the 1979 set.

Don't bend any of the corners, Dead Paul said. Most of the corners were already bent. Even the cards that weren't bent had black mold creeping in from the edges.

"These are all messed up. You don't even have them in any order or anything," he said.

Dead Paul just waited with his mouth open. After shuffling through the shoebox for a few minutes, Paul got bored and wiped his hands on what looked like a dry spot on the bedspread. The fabric was brittle and frayed when he wiped the goop off his hands.

"Do you have any games? Puzzles?" he asked Dead Paul. As he stood on tiptoe to reach the boxes in the back of the closet shelves, the surrounding shadows shifted and skittered away. He ignored it, but the hair prickled on his arms with the certainty that the things he couldn't see wanted to be close to him. He pretended the chewing noises came from the television in the living room.

"Do things ever come out of the walls to get you in here?" Paul asked. His voice quavered and he cleared his throat to cover it. He tried not to let on how much he wanted to run back down the hallway and out the door. Back up to the sunlight and breeze in his backyard.

No, only down in the basement. Sometimes gross things crawl out of the floor down there, Dead Paul said. *But you don't have to go down there if you're scared.*

Dead Paul smirked from the bed.

Paul was determined to show him he wasn't afraid of the stupid basement. His whole house smelled like garbage and his parents were dead and stupid, just like him. "Are you going to get up and come with me down there, or do you want me to carry you down there?"

I'm already in the basement, waiting for you, Dead Paul said, and it was true. When Paul glanced over the bed, it was empty. The rumpled bedspread showed where Dead Paul had been lying before. It was less faded in the center, like a chalk outline from a crime show, but in child-sized proportions.

The padlock on the basement door hung open on its latch. Pauls' real, living parents always kept the basement door locked. Paul crept down the stairs to the basement. The single light bulb was almost worse than the dark. It cast shadows in all the corners and small noises made him jump. Too soon he stood on the packed dirt floor and the small scratching noises filled every corner. Paul couldn't tell if they were digging to get in or to escape. "Where are you?"

I'm under here. Where did you think I was going to be? Dead Paul's voice came from under the floor. *Do you hear that? Something's trying to get in to eat you. Nothing scratched the walls to get in before you got here.*

"Ok, I'm going to go home now. Maybe I'll come back next week with some new c-comics," Paul said. The scratching stopped, but there was a new pressure in the room. The weight of watching eyes settled onto him. Every shadow could be a crouched figure, waiting to jump. "I'll see you later."

He didn't move, though, despite how much his mind screamed to bolt, to flee in a blind panic. He wanted to tear up the stairs flailing at the unseen watchers, to scramble breathlessly through the kitchen, out the side door, and back up the steps he'd uncovered. Out into the sunlight and the sky and the trees with singing birds. But he didn't; the shifting shadows kept him rooted to the spot.

They want you to run so they can catch you. Get the shovel and dig me up and we can trade places. They won't catch you unless you run. Dead

Paul didn't sound scared at all. No hitch in his words, no tremble in his voice.

Paul took up the shovel for the second time that day and started digging. It didn't take long to uncover Dead Paul, though he did accidentally gouge his arm pretty hard with the shovel.

"S-sorry, I didn't mean to h-hurt your arm," he said and wiped his eyes. He estimated the steps out of the basement and how long it might take to run all of them.

I didn't feel anything; I'm dead, remember? Now get in the hole, Dead Paul said. *We're trading places. I'll come back in a week or two with some new comics, or baseball cards that aren't all moldy.*

Where before Dead Paul had only lay still, now he scampered on all fours, scraping his hands and feet across the dirt. He slid in and out of the shadows and the scratching, chewing noises surrounded Paul. He didn't know where to turn.

Get in the hole! You're staying here and I'm going to take your place. I want to go to school, practice soccer, and eat birthday cake. Dead Paul pushed him from behind.

Paul cried out and lost his balance.

Dead Paul shoved him, again and again, until he fell in the hole. He'd grown tired of being dead and missing out on everything.

"But I don't want to stay down here. Do I have to be dead?" Paul screamed and tried to scramble out of the hole, but the sides collapsed, and he slid back down. The first shovel full of dirt landed heavy on his head and some got in his eyes, turning his tears to mud. "You tricked me!"

Being dead doesn't hurt, Dead Paul said. *It's just boring. Mom and Dad are dead, and so is Chubbles, and everything else down here.* The hole disappeared, one shovelful of dirt at a time. After the hole was filled in, Dead Paul kicked dirt around and stomped down the edges.

He didn't want either of his parents to see the hole with Paul down here, not that they ever left the kitchen. He turned the one light bulb off and ignored the scrabbling, crawling whispers from the dark corners of the basement. He climbed the stairs and locked the door behind him.

"I'm going back to my house now, Dad and Mom," New Paul said as he walked through the kitchen on his way out. He turned explanations for how he'd hurt his arm over in his mind, even though it wasn't bleeding much now. "I'll just say I cut it while I was digging the hole for Chubbles and ask for a new gerbil."

Chubbles is dead. The new gerbil will die, too, Dead Paul said from the basement. *Mom and Dad, Grandma, and you, too. One day, your picture will be on the wall in the hallway. Go have all the fun you can, but one day I'll see you down here again.*

He climbed back up and out of the hole, into the back yard. He covered his eyes; he'd never been in the sunshine before or seen the sky or trees with singing birds. The backyard was warm, with a life of its own, and New Paul decided he'd never go back down in the dark ever again.

Fall on Me

Mother fainted on the table after breakfast with her hand still over her mouth from coughing. That same morning, I found the first piece of rail in our backyard. This was before everyone else started complaining about the rails and we didn't know what it meant, yet.

Father acted like none of us kids noticed the blood on her lips, but I did. He carried her back to their room to put her to bed. "Mama's tired, kids. Let her rest. Meadow, take your sisters and make sure the laundry is brought off the line."

Harmony and River held hands and twirled in circles until they fell down laughing. They rolled over each other and smashed dandelions and fleabane until their elbows were green, and delicate yellow and white petals clung in their hair. I wasn't going to ask them to help with the laundry, or I'd have to wash it all over again.

I stopped short when I banged my toe on what I thought was a root growing out of the grass. I'd hung laundry more than a hundred times, and it wasn't there before today, or I would have tripped over it. I squatted down and shifted the laundry basket around to investigate. It wasn't a root at all, but a piece of steel, burnished and shining, that broke out of the soil. About three feet of rail arched out of the ground and while I watched, more crept up through the sod on either end of the exposed bit.

I've seen railed-road tracks before, with Mother and Father when we went walking down to the river on the other side of the village. This was before Harmony and River were even born. I wanted to see where Father unloaded boats when I was little. He pointed out the road over the water.

"That's a railed-road bridge, Meadow. There used to be men who drove great, long worms over those carrying coal, and carts, and sometimes cows, too." He said it all with a straight face, but I could tell he was trying to trick me.

"A worm can't carry a cart or a cow, Daddy!" I saw him nudge Mother to make her smile. She used to smile and braid lavender into my hair to make it smell pretty. I'd wanted her to braid lavender into my hair the day she got sick. I could never do it right by myself.

"It was a really big worm, Meadow. And they trained them to roll on wheels on the railed-road. My grandpa told me you could put your hand on the rail and feel it shaking when a trained worm was coming."

We walked that day, right up to the edge of the bridge over the water, but there was nothing left of the tracks. So much of the metal for the bridge had been scavenged by then, too, that it was barely still there. People needed it for other things, Mother told me.

Daddy showed me a picture book when we got home. He'd kept it hidden in a cupboard. The book was full of brittle pages with pictures of all kinds of different trains. He told me what all the different pieces were called. For months after, I mumbled them to myself every night as I fell asleep.

"Cattle-catcher. Cylinder. Steam chest. Running board. Smoke-stack." And then I'd dream of railed-road tracks circling the whole village, only everyone was angry at me for it. The whole village gathered in my dreams after that, and they refused to forgive me. They all pointed and shouted, no matter where I tried to hide.

"Machines lead to sloth, Meadow! You've damned us all!"

After that, Daddy never showed me the precious train book full of its forbidden machines again, but he didn't need to; I never forgot any of the pictures of the different locomotives, diesels, and electric engines. And so I knew what it was when I stubbed my toe on the piece of track. *This a railed-road track for the trained worm.*

I put my hand on the rail section that raised up out of the ground, but it wasn't the rail shaking. My hand shook, remembering Mother coughing and the red stains spreading on her handkerchief. I knew what it meant for her, for me, and Father.

I was supposed to go and meet Elliott Paul down by the river later that day. He'd been asking me places, just the two of us, but then he'd get tongue-tied and blush when we were alone. I think he was working up the nerve to try and kiss me and I'd always get butterflies in my stomach until it was tied up in knots. But I couldn't imagine kissing him later; after seeing Mother faint, I couldn't unknot my stomach for a completely separate reason.

Harmony and River had stopped playing and both stood there, squinting down at me.

"I thought we were getting the laundry, Meadow. Why are you crying?"

By the next week, Mother couldn't get out of bed at all, and the railed-road tracks had broken through the ground all over the village. More than a dozen sets crisscrossed the farms and fields, plus one pair popped out of the ground right through the Assembly Hall. The bricks crumbled where the steel cut through the wall, and the rails divided the meeting room into two equal halves.

The ones behind our house stretched all the way past the forest. I finished my chores and walked along beside them until I was tired of walking and sat down. I didn't worry about getting lost since I could turn around and follow the rails back to our house. I rested my hand on the rail and waited to feel something.

I went down to the Assembly Hall with Father to meet with everyone else in the village yesterday. Almost the whole village was there, except for Grandmother Willoughby who was too old to walk very far anymore. And Mother. Harmony and River wound string around each other's fingers and giggled while the complaints started. We arrived last and the other men nodded to Father, or slapped him on the shoulder.

"Sorry to hear it, Daniel," they all said, but they never said what *it* was.

None of them said my mother's name.

"Well, someone's got to do something! Where'd these damn things even come from, that's what I want to know? I can't have 'em running through the middle of the corn and beans!" Aron Fogelman twisted his hands together with a sound like sand turning in the scouring bucket. "The cows won't cross over them and we've broken two cart wheels already."

I leaned over to whisper to Father, "Does Mr. Fogelman even grow beans, Daddy?" I hoped to see him grin and nudge me in the ribs with his elbow, but he only gave me a small look. More gray grew into his beard than was there at his last birthday and his eyes were sunk down in his face. His smile was a ghost, but he didn't shush me like he used to do when I was small like River.

I balled my fists and my arms shook with my stifled sense of unfairness. Mother's sickness. The railedroad tracks turning everything
inside out. All of it. I wanted to stomp my feet. Screams boiled and
got caught in my throat until I yearned to get up and kick the stupid
railed-road track until it melted back into the ground where it came
from.

I almost went over to Daisy Merrill and pulled her hair like I did
back when we were in lessons together. She still gave me a wary look
even now, but it was ten years since I taught her to stop pinching her
face up at me. Now if we catch each other's eyes, she only looks away;
she doesn't even purse her lips where I can see it.

"How often do crops need to be rotated?" That was the question
our old teacher Ms. Simpkins had just asked and Daisy made that ugly,
sneering face she made every time I raised my hand. Instead of telling
Ms. Simpkins, *"A six-year rotation allows for the right balance of soil
nutrients,"* I reached over and pulled Daisy out of her chair by her
stupid ponytail. Mother sat me down for a talking to over that, and
Father gave me extra chores for a week, but Daisy didn't make that face
ever again.

"I'll do all the extra chores, Daddy!" I blurted out, and my feet
thumped on the wooden floor when I stood up. "I'll do all the extra
chores, and I'll do something about the locomotive tracks, too. Just
—you tell me what— and get Mama up... and you make her..." I
stopped because I couldn't see straight. I wiped my eyes and took a
deep breath, ready to demand that Father do something. My embarrassment burned on my cheeks. The room stayed dead quiet while
everyone's faces came into focus through my hot tears; they all stared
at me and my anger immediately evaporated. I sat and buried my face
in my father's shoulder. No one said anything until Mr. Fogelman
cleared his throat.

"Loco-what now?" Mr. Fogelman turned to Father.

"She means trains, Farmer Fogelman. It's an old story I told her when she was young." Father stood to address everyone, but his shoulders slumped. "They're called train tracks. My own grandfather told me about them. They used to have big machines that hauled all kinds of things for people on the railed-roads."

Some of the men shifted in their seats at the mention of machines. They glanced at each other, and then at the rail sticking up out of the floor. *Machines lead to sloth, and sloth leads to ruin.* They may as well have said it, even though the adults had all agreed to stop the teachings. No one had time for church anymore anyhow; chores didn't do themselves.

"Not all machines were the same, I see the look on your faces, Jared, Aron, and the rest of you." Father turned to face the other men and women. Their mouths turned down in frowns of sympathy, but Father held his hands out to the rails on the floor and shrugged his shoulders. "But I don't know what this is. We've seen the land do peculiar things, and it'll do what it wants, so I don't know what we do about this. Them rails are steel, and thick."

The same men who'd made puckered faces at the mention of machines widened their eyes and leaned forward at the mention of steel. "Steel? Are you telling it true, Daniel? All them tracks that sprouted up are made of the same?"

Father nodded, but the others buzzed with plans.

"We need a plank for prying. If we can bend it up out of the ground far enough, it might break a piece off. Steel! Wait'll we bring this to the Council of Grandmothers!" All the other farmers and stevedores huddled together over the rail in the middle of the room, but Father beckoned to me to gather River and Harmony, like they had always been my responsibility.

We walked home under a full moon and its silver smile glinted off the train tracks in every direction. Parallel flashes of bright steel laced through and around everything in the village.

"Why are there train tracks now, Daddy?" It was a demand, not a question. I needed him to give me answers. *Explain it, Daddy. You always know why the world is the way it is, don't you?*

River and Harmony took turns trying to jump from one rail to the other and laughed when they couldn't make it.

"Sometimes the old things come back, sweetie. I don't know why it happens, but there's not much we can do about it." Father pointed down the track. "Looks like if we follow this one, it'll lead us to the house."

On the way, my sisters made up a contest to see who could balance on only one of the rails the longest. They were so funny, yelling and jumping off when they lost their balance, that Father and I tried their game too. Father's boots slipped off the rail after his third step, but not mine.

I kept my balance all the way home.

That night, after the meeting, Father called me into the room with Mother. She shivered on her pallet next to the fireplace. A huge pile of logs roared with tongues of flame and the air around her shimmered.

"Meadow, you make sure your sisters learn something more than how to marry a stevedore." Mother's voice belonged to a mouse. Too wispy, and nothing at all like the voice she used to sing, back before she coughed. Father smiled down at her and bent to sit on the floor next to her.

"You did ok marrying one," he said, but his words met the air like bees from a smoked hive. Both of them were too small, down there on the floor, and Father's soaked shirt showed his ribs. They were both dying; Mama would die from the coughing-sick and then Father would just wither away. From his broken heart.

They'd leave me to raise my sisters and the only thing she'd told me was to make sure they didn't marry stevedores. No advice on what it means when a man can't speak when you look him in the eye, and whether to lie down or squat when you're giving birth. Just half a piece of stale wisdom before they were ignoring me altogether, like I didn't need her just as much as my father and my sisters.

Harmony and River would probably forget all about her by the time they were my age. I already knew who would be expected to tell them what getting their blood meant, and what to do when a boy wants a kiss, or more. I'd fill that place in their lives instead of her. They'd think of *me* as their Mama.

While Father leaned over and kissed Mother's sweat-slicked forehead, I imagined leaving in the morning. I wouldn't have to stay and watch them die if I left. I'd go down to the river and climb onto the next flat-decked crate boat that docked. I could work as hard as any of the boys in the village, plus I knew everything you could learn about farming here.

If that didn't work, I could run away with Elliott Paul. He kept trying to give me his grandmother's ring. Him and a few other men in town stopped working if my errands carried me by. I knew the picture I made to them; I looked just like Mother. They all used to look at her and lick their lips. Their eyebrows would scrunch like they were concentrating, or confused.

When Father's shoulders shook, I tiptoed out of the room and lay on my pallet at the other end of the house. The girls were already asleep. That first set of soot-stained train tracks I'd found cut through the house now, right between my bed and theirs. They were on one side of the divided room, asleep and not at all worried about how they'd grow up or who would braid their hair. My heart ached to join them, to nestle in with them, but my anger held me fast. I wanted something of my own, even if I had to walk until I was someone new in some other village to get it.

I could've packed up my clothes, taken some buttered bread, and eased the train book out of its hiding place, all without waking up my sisters or stirring Father's attention right then, but instead I lay down and stared at the ceiling, wishing it would fall on me.

✤

I didn't do any chores the next morning, and I didn't pack anything. I woke up and started walking. But instead of going to the river and climbing aboard a boat, I made up my mind and followed the rail until I got to wherever it started. Or ended.

I'd marched past the Assembly Hall, past the fields where Farmer Fogelman didn't grow beans, and all the way out of the village. I walked until I got tired of walking, and then I sat down. I grieved for my mama, and my daddy, and the way Elliott Paul looked at me, because I wanted him to tell me what came after it.

I sat with my hand on the sun-warm rail for a few minutes, but then remembered my mama's face when she told me to make sure my sisters learned.

I remembered my father's ribs sticking out under his shirt.

Harmony and River would have to grow up and take care of Father in a house without our mama. They'd have to help him out of his bed and feed him from their plates and then he'd go and die on them anyway.

I don't know if I changed my mind because of my daddy, or for my sisters, but before I started back along the tracks, a cloud of black ribbon drifted diagonally toward the ground across the field from the forest. It wasn't the same as when the fields were burned after the harvest; this was just one finger of smoke trailing closer.

I leaned on the rail and shaded my eyes. The ribbon smoked and billowed and trailed from a gleaming black cart on silver wheels.

Is that cart on fire? The answer came from under my hand. The rail shivered against my palm.

A train!

I stumbled back along the rail, looking over my shoulder for the demon machine; certain the train would catch me and do whatever machines did when they caught teenage girls who'd abandoned their families. I'd never see Mama and Daddy again.

As I fled, another plume of smoke rose, and then another. A shrill scream drifted on the wind, high-pitched and terrifying. A flock of starlings burst into the sky from the field; there were more trains than I could count. Pealing bells rang over and over as they chugged toward the village.

I peered over my shoulder and a steaming black barrel on huge wooden driving wheels bore down on me. A menacing cattle-catcher rattled on the front of the locomotive, and I covered my ears as the smoking, hissing calamity overtook me.

It let out another roaring belch of smoke and a screaming-mad whistle right as it smashed into the Assembly Hall and burst into flames. The train derailed on impact and the coal bunker behind it plowed end-over-end through the top of the building. A black cloud of coal dust flew into the sky and the fire pouring out of the side of the engine ignited it. The sky itself exploded and the roar sent me sprawling in the grass.

My ears rang, and the acrid smell of my burned hair clouded my mind, but I dragged myself up and pounded in the direction of home. More trains barreled into houses, or roared by, trailing cars on squealing wheels. I pounded faster on throbbing feet. I'd get to the house and Daddy would know what to do, he'd sweep me up in his arms and everything would be safe again, even if Mama was still sick.

Even when she died, Harmony and River and Daddy and me would still carry her. We could talk about her and love her and remember all the small things she did for everyone in the village. She would always be with us.

"Remember when Mama would sing for us when she did the washing?" we will ask each other, and still be able to hear her singing, then. I'll sing all her songs, and when I marry Elliott Paul, or some other man with strong arms and kind eyes, we'll have a daughter and name her Lavender.

I'll teach her all the songs my mother sang.

While I ran, I dreamed a whole future for my daughter full of laughing cousins and her grandpa doting on her. And in her future, the land would keep all the trains and railed-roads buried deep down where they couldn't ever come back. No one got the coughing sickness that grew in lumps and stole the breath right out of your chest.

I ran toward my mama, picturing her getting better and braiding her granddaughter's hair with lavender so it smelled pretty.

I believed in that future for my daughter named Lavender, for one more moment after the wall of the house exploded in a cloud of splinters and brick dust. An orange electric freight engine barreled out of the house on the rails that had sprouted up through the backyard. Its horn screamed a too-late warning and I joined it, screaming for my mother.

Our house collapsed and disintegrated under the wheels of the impossibly long train, its cars laden with coal, carts, and lowing cows. I stopped and dropped to the ground, and even the earth itself rumbled with the lumbering progress of the trains. They'd come and taken everything from me. The whole village smoked and crumbled; people cried out from every direction. I should have gotten up and tried to help. I could have done even some small thing, but instead I lay down, staring at the sky, wishing it would fall on me.

Home to Mexico

M y leather pouch spilled gold nuggets and my partner Digsy lay on the ground in pieces. We'd never found gold. Neither of us knew much about being out in the scrub or the actual work of mining. Except for our merchandise, I'd never even held any of the tools. The first time either of us had swung a pick was to nestle the dynamite in the rock.

That's how we found the cave. The hole we blew in the rock whistled, low and mournful. It groaned like the worst kind of sadness, the sounds a man makes when he's defeated, nothing left to lose. Those were the times we lived in; fortunes were made and lost equally fast.

"I didn't hear no wind before we blew it open," Digsy said, scratching his head, his other hand on his hip. He never was good at putting the simple things together, but he'd made a great partner for our enterprise. Never met another man with a head for sums like him. Between the two of us, we'd struck it rich selling canned meat, shovels, and wire screens.

"Weren't gonna be no wind until we blew the other end open, Digsy." We both stood there, peering down at the hole and lingering over the moaning coming out of it.

I sure wish we hadn't gone in.

"Well, I reckon we should go in. Don't you think so, Bill?" Digsy hitched his pack and waited for me to answer.

"We come out to stake a claim, right? Gold's nice, but it ain't all there is. Might be silver or amethyst down there, maybe. Let's climb in and see what we find. I hope it ain't bears." I climbed in headfirst and Digsy followed. I wanted him to have a little fun, get a taste of this sort of thing, a real man's work one busted prospector called it, before we headed back home. We'd been so busy for the last year, neither one of us had time to do much more than eat and sleep outside of running the shop. We sold twenty-cent screening pans for ten dollars, and a two-dollar shovel fetched fifteen due to gold fever.

"Bears live underground, Bill? In caves?" He'd believe me if I said so.

"I think they only sleep in 'em to overwinter. Best not to worry ahead." We lit our lamps and got a look around. Past the mouth, the cave opened into a gaping passage. I couldn't touch either wall from the middle.

Digsy leaned close, squinting at the wall. "These is smooth, Bill. Something scraped all the rough edges off. You ever seen anything like this?"

I didn't have to lean in to see he was right. The rock walls were grooved, but uniformly smooth. "Nah, nothing like this. No struts or rafters, either."

Digsy studied the cave, running his hands over the walls, floor, and ceiling, frowning while he tried to puzzle it out. "You want to see where it goes?" He asked it like he was shrugging, figuring the worst outcome might be a few wasted hours. I wish I'd said no and turned us right around, but I didn't.

"Might as well, right? Maybe we'll find out who made the tunnel. Still may find something worthwhile, too."

We'd come through the Nevada territory, following the same rumors and stories as the flocks of broke-dick prospectors and all their fleas. But we'd set up a shop instead, and we'd done fine for ourselves. We'd taken claims in trade and sold our business to a fellow from Missouri with plans for a rooming house once the claims were all played out.

A few men got lucky-rich, but more of them starved in the backcountry with nothing to show for their efforts but their ribs poking out of their scrawny chests. Before we carried on home to Kansas, we come out to this claim for the fun of it. Nothing at stake, so we pushed on out of curiosity.

The path sloped gently downward, and the walls kept the same uniform groove the farther we went. Our footsteps didn't echo, instead every sound we made died in the confines of the tunnel. But the light from our lamps lit the whole corridor for at least twenty feet in front of us, not that there was anything to see. Same ahead as behind.

"How far you think it goes?" Digsy's eyes rolled back and forth while we trudged.

"Why are you whispering, Digsy? This ain't church."

He grinned abashedly, but when he spoke again, it was the same hushed tones. "Dunno, just felt right to be respectful, Bill. I don't know whose house this is and all."

Digsy's comment raised the hair on my neck and I stopped mid-step. I didn't know why Digsy's comment unsettled me so. "Why'd you say a damn fool thing like that, Digsy?"

"Well, I don't know. I'm sorry, Bill." He hitched his pack up on his shoulders again and then he froze, too. "You hear that?"

My breath hitched in my chest while the unease settled into me nice and deep, but I didn't hear anything except the wind in the passage. "I don't hear nothing new."

"Someone's in trouble, Bill!" Before I could stop him, Digsy charged down the passage. Between the tools and pans in his pack and his stomping like a damn fool, he made so much noise people the next county over knew we were coming. To my shame, I let him run ahead until I was sure there was enough distance between us that I could turn tail and run back to safety if robbers jumped out of the shadows. A fear was upon me like I've never known, like someone could see right into my thoughts. I stood, rooted to the spot for a moment and I almost turned back the way we'd come and left Digsy down there to fend for himself. I steeled my nerves, though, and followed him. I stripped off my own pack and tried to run quietly, all the while the finger of someone else's notions stirred in my mind. They weren't human, these thoughts, and for a fleeting moment, I forgot who I was. The feeling passed and I shook the chill from my mind with a force of will.

I caught up with him at the entrance to a larger cavern that branched off to one side. I crept closer, keeping about ten feet between us, with my lantern screened. I shuddered at the voices, dozens of them, reciting the Lord's prayer. Some keened and wailed the words, others sang them out with joy. Confused, I didn't know whether I'd peer into the cavern and perhaps find some foul witchcraft, or if there was really a church down here underground.

"Hallowed be thy name." An entire chorus sang, and I've never heard a worse sound. Hundreds of people were crying out to the Lord for rescue, and it sounded like they all knew it weren't coming. "Thy kingdom come, thy will be done."

Digsy dropped his pack on the floor of the passage and rooted around in it until he pulled out his three-pound hammer. He never glanced back at me; he might have forgotten I was there. He brandished his hammer in one hand and his lantern in the other. He shouted while he walked down the path into the larger cavern below. "Hey there! You leave those people be! Turn 'em loose now!"

I dropped to my hands and knees and crawled toward the mouth of the cave to see what he was doing. I still can't be sure of what I beheld, but it wasn't a cave. It was all lit up like daylight from glowing rectangles spaced evenly along the ceiling above rows of gleaming tables. Men in robes stood along the tables, but it wasn't immediately apparent what they were up to. In front of each of them lay the body of a man, woman, or child and all in various states of completion. Some of them lacked hair, or legs, but however it came to be here, the product of this cavern's workmen was people. The completed humans milled about a cordoned off platform, reciting the prayer. Workmen moved between them, adjusting clothes, posture, or working tools that changed the people's voices.

Digsy dropped his lantern and approached the nearest workman. I hadn't paid any mind to them. I was so captivated by their work, that I failed to notice they had some kind of octopus in place of a head, and gray skin. Digsy grabbed the workman by the shoulder, and the foul monster caught his wrist with inhuman speed and embraced him. I realized the thing's tentacles had wrapped around his face. It wasn't until Digsy struck with his hammer that the octopus-man fell and Digsy wiped at the black goop coating his face and neck where the tentacles touched him. More of the octopus men left their places at the tables while Digsy clambered up the roped off platform. A half-finished man lay on the table where the fallen monster had been working. The man had arms and legs, but no chest or stomach. Instead, his insides were exposed, devoid of blood or ichor.

Digsy jostled the closest person, a tall, gaunt man with a shock of white hair under a top hat. He shook the stranger by the shoulder, but he never stopped his recitations, even when Digsy screamed right in his face. "Come on, fella, we have to get out of here! Get moving, now!"

I prayed silently that Digsy wouldn't call out to me. I dropped down to my belly and lay there, frozen.

The octomonster men were almost to him now, and Digsy let go of the man to swing his hammer. When they came close enough, he bashed them with his hammer, but they didn't stay down. They somersaulted and crawled after him. Before long, and despite his valiant effort, they surrounded and overpowered Digsy.

None of the people reciting the prayer in the roped off section of the room even glanced over at the commotion or stopped in their prayer. They finished and then started over. All manner of men and women stood there together, too; a railroad laborer, a *vaquero*, and a churched-up white woman in a dress and hat all stood shoulder to shoulder staring straight ahead while they recited. Not a flicker of life shone in their eyes, any of them.

I swear I meant to get up and go help Digsy, but just when I'd decided to pull myself up off the ground, a rush of air filled my head like someone blowing out a candle. The whole world was only darkness, but I wasn't asleep at first. I couldn't open my eyes, and I couldn't move, but I was aware of the hands that picked me up. They must have had thorns or claws, because their grip tore my skin, and burned something fierce., I blacked out completely, but I'll never forget the squeaky, guttered words those octopus-headed men said to each other, even if I don't know what they meant.

I woke under a canopy of twinkling stars, back outside and Digsy was in pieces on the ground around me. I rolled away, screaming, and landed with my hip on the lumpy pouch on my belt. Dust billowed off my clothes, far older and more worn than the brand-new stiff denims I'd been wearing before. My screams tapered off and I fumbled the pouch out from under me. I opened it and gold spilled out, more than anyone ever brought into our shop at once, maybe a few hundred dollars' worth. Nuggets tumbled into my palm, and I struggled to make sense of my new situation.

"Mi nombre es Bill, no?" I asked, unsure now myself. "Oh Dios, dónde estoy?" Like waking from a dream, all my memories of myself, of Bill, faded. I tried to hold onto some of it, who I was...who I'd been my whole life, but it was no good.

I didn't remember how I got here, but I knew I should find my mules and head back to Tijuana before someone came along and tried to pin this dismembered white man on me. I whistled softly for Petey and Camel and tied my pouch back to my belt. If I could make it home without getting waylaid, I wouldn't have to scrabble like a dog just to make it to tomorrow. I knew most people who came to California left with less, but not me. I'd found a good vein of rotten quartz spilling over with nuggets. If I could find those damn mules, I'd be that much closer to home. I whistled again, hoisted my pack, and started walking home to Mexico.

Salvation and Final Judgment

James waited to dig a grave for himself last. By the second day after the last villager died, he'd been through every cupboard in the church twice over. The food was all gone, even the sacramental bread and wine. No more Jesus at all—James had eaten His last crumbs and drunk the last cup of Him down to the dregs.

James passed the first day after everyone else died stacking gold coins on the stone steps of the churchyard; he could stack them as high as his knee before they fell over. He'd had precious little gold while performing his backbreaking labors—hunching and scraping—and no thanks besides.

Now that he could have all the gold he wanted, the dead rotted in their homes or in the lanes where they had fallen. His buboes had festered into hard lumps and every movement pained him, and so he abandoned his stacks of gold.

James stayed in the church long past the end of the food because of the monstrous goat. It prowled the village, pounding the cobbles with its great black hooves, sending up sparks and smoke smelling of foul brimstone. If James passed by the open doorway, or peeked from around an empty window sash, the goat's eyes were on him. Its gaze bored into him, and he knew in the depths of his soul that he was damned. All of them were, the dead and the buried alike. So he slunk and hid in the church, pretending he was content to scuttle and scrape and scour the pews with his fitful rest. and avoiding the goat's regard whenever possible.

"T'weren't the Lord's fault the cupboard run empty," James whispered as he prowled the church. Now that it was only him, he could talk to himself without fear of the priest cuffing him behind the ear. The priest, a mean-hearted Italian named Giacomo Bertolli, had always raised a hand to James no matter what task he'd been set to around the churchyard. But now the priest lay black and shriveling in his cloister. He would never cuff anyone again.

"The devil is in your whispers, Wesselshire!" James shouted from the pulpit and cackled. "Damnation awaits! The sickness took you all and left only James, God's chosen, to walk the path of Bonfil ius!" James didn't really know anything about Bonfilius save that he'd arrived in Jerusalem alone after all his companions died. "And now James will starve while God reserves the power to grant life!"

He'd smashed all the stained glass for fun and made a bed nest out of vestments because they were softer than straw. When he caught a chill, he burned pages from the Bible in the baptismal font. It was the most benefit he'd gotten from the word of the Lord in his whole life, and the chill sank back into his bones once the pages were all gone.

He'd eaten the leather cover, tearing it into strips and chewing each one a hundred times, but that was a week past now, and his hunger lingered. He imagined all the fingers that had ever touched the leather, and eating those, too. All the chewing made his neck stiff, and the leather clogged his throat, gagging him. No amount of retching made it go away, instead it was like having a stone lodged in his windpipe. He'd wheezed and coughed, since.

James thought of all the people in the village and what each of them had done to earn God's wrath. He couldn't imagine that Daniel the butcher, Matthew the fisherman, and Rastus the stonemason had all been covetous enough to deserve their deaths. Not to mention the serving girls at the manor house like his sister Ruth, or her daughter Mary. James couldn't imagine a babe of four months offending the Lord enough to deserve her fate. So much of the evidence at hand was hard to swallow, but God had seen to it that each of them was smote by His hand.

On the third day, with nothing left in the church to eat, and nothing else to smash and tinkle for fun, James hefted his grave-digging shovel over his shoulder and limped and staggered and crawled up the road to the manor house on the hill.

Aside from the church, it was the only building in the village with glass windows and a tile roof. The lord there had worn silk and fur, nothing at all like James's own roughspun work clothes. When he was a younger lad, he'd daydreamed of lying in wait on the road out of the village and robbing the lord of the manor, thus starting his life as a daring bandit. His fantasies suffocated under a life of toil in and around the church, though, and he gave up on ever being a successful highwayman. With a grieving heart, he'd abandoned all the gold at the church; its burdensome weight was too great and he couldn't eat it, besides. Upon reflection, he was puzzled why he'd ever coveted it in the first place.

"Hey ho! James the Lord of the Manor is arrived! Fetch my mutton and ale, cuff the servants," he called out in the doorway. A corpse greeted him, the previous lord of the manor who lay black and swollen on the floor of the sitting room.

"Do you still desire my riches, James? I am clad in finery, and you're still covered in muck!"

"Nah, you're dead, and dead things don't talk," James said.

The lord hooted with brittle laughter, but James ignored him and explored the fine house. He found a dusty bottle of wine and three more bloated corpses, but no food. Whether a servant packed in a sack to flee in desperation, James didn't know, but the pantries and cupboards were all bare except for a layer of fine dust. He even dragged the cookpot out of the fireplace and tried to lower his head into it to lick the bottom, but tasted only the tang of cold cast iron, gritty with rust.

He drowned himself in the wine and sang all the bawdy songs he could remember. When the wine was all drunk, he bellowed a new song.

> "The lord of the manor, so fat and rich,
> Poor old James, digs a ditch,
> Now endless riches James has got,
> But a feast for a beggar, he has not,
> He'll starve to death before Christ comes back,
> But the lord of the manor is still dead and black!"

James sang his song until he croaked out the words, and then vomited on himself before passing out in the empty pantry.

He slept and dreamt of the great black goat, and now it followed him everywhere. It waited for him to die, and then it would eat him. James grabbed it up and shook it, for he was not afraid anymore, but the goat refused to speak to him. It only blinked its slit-pupiled eyes at him.

When he woke again, the darkness was absolute. Even the moon and stars had died while he slept. No more Jesus, no more priest's cuffing, and no more light from the heavens. James dragged himself along the floor and wailed in his despair. "If I'm to live in the darkness, at least leave me a scrap of food! A morsel of bread, or even a slow rat." But there weren't any rats left in the village.

James crawled around the house, twice blundering into the corpses and sinking his hands through their soft, pliant flesh. They rose to creep in the darkness, despite being dead and stiff, and moved to block his way. Their stifled laughter taunted him. It leaked out of them in a putrid cloud, their skins splitting from the effort of containing their mirth. The stale air smelled of rot and sweetness, but the corpses kept up their giggles. Every time he moved, they danced out of reach and whispered the secrets of the dead. "There's no heaven and no hell, James. There's only cold dirt and worms and the quiet of the grave. There aren't any prayers and no more promises of salvation because God isn't watching."

"You'll not keep me in this charnel house! I'll find a flint and burn us all to hell if you don't leave me be!" He strained to listen for crawling, or the hint of a corpse creeping, but the house stood still and silent. The dead rested again, but better to be on his guard. James fetched up in a corner and closed his eyes. All the crawling in the pitch dark made his knees throb. He considered praying to spite the teasing dead that danced around the house but didn't know the words for a proper prayer, and they were probably right, besides. God didn't look down on Wesselshire any longer. The village lost His regard and now it was dead, except for James. James gave up the idea of praying. "'Tis useless," he said.

James woke in the garden behind the manor house with no memory of how he got there, but he'd been kicked by the horrible dream-goat in his sleep. Bruises colored his ribs and groin and every new breath pained him. Filth covered every bit of his breeches and tunic, so he stripped them off and staggered naked back into the manor house to find new clothes.

"Hey ho, the Lord of the Manor needs dressing! Fetch the maids to my dressing room," he called, but his rasping words died in the dim quiet. He stomped through the rooms until he found clothing and pulled an old shift over his shoulders. No one remained to be scandalized if he dressed in women's clothes and the loose fit sat nicer on his swollen neck and groin. His stomach rumbled. His strength faded. His arms and legs dragged him down into the mud again, where the hunger settled into every joint. It rode his thoughts and lashed him with its barbs, constantly. He tried to clear his head, but his thoughts droned on, full of juicy capons, roasted lamb, and stewed carrots.

The goat from his dreams the night before watched him from the top of the hill, but James didn't entertain any idea of trying to catch and eat it. Its horns curled menacingly over its brow and its powerful legs ended in sharp-edged hooves. It was no ordinary goat; no, this one's flesh was misery and its blood was cold greed. If he came close enough to touch it, it would surely destroy him.

"If I'm to starve, I'll dig me a grave so I can tumble in and rest until the final judgment," James said and set to digging a grave for himself in the garden. "You'll not eat old James, you goat-footed bastard child of hellspawn!" He dug in the first flat patch of ground he came upon. James had dug plenty of graves, sometimes burying a dozen or more plague victims in one hole, and he had his own grave roughed out. The digging took longer because his joints ached, his head throbbed, and his confused mind wandered back to the goat watching from the hill. Once knee deep in his own grave, he climbed laboriously out of the hole to squint around, but the goat had hidden away again. "Keep away from me, foul creature."

James put his shovel to the dirt again and struck something solid. The impact sent a painful shiver up his arms and the wooden head on his shovel snapped in half. He used his half-shovel to scrape away dirt from around whatever he'd struck and found a shining, enameled bit of metalwork. James gawped at it, curious if he'd uncovered a doorway to hell itself. Given the circumstances, it wouldn't have surprised him any and if they had food down in those eternal flames, James would walk through willingly. Using his hands to scoop away more dirt, James uncovered more of the metal, revealing a strip of chrome, too. He clawed and tossed the dirt over his shoulder until he uncovered a shining rectangle that showed him his own face.

"What witchcraft is this?" James pawed at his loosened, jowly cheeks, and the smaller version of himself in the mirror did the same. Even though he might be risking the theft of his very soul, he couldn't stop staring. Somehow, he'd been captured and imprisoned in the rectangle and he had to break himself out. With his fading strength, he swung the remnants of his shovel at the tiny prison until he managed to shatter the glass. Horror overwhelmed him when he gazed into the silvered reflection again and saw he'd only succeeded in breaking himself up into countless tiny prisons. His mind swam, and he wanted more than anything to simply lie down and sleep, but the mystery of his discovery compelled him to keep digging.

James scraped and panted until he uncovered more of the metal. He ran his fingers over the crest, caressing shining letters one at a time, though he couldn't read them. C-A-D-I-L-L-A-C. Reinvigorated, he cleared away more dirt. James' frantic scrabbling stopped when he uncovered enough of the window to see into the chamber, and the man sitting in the leather driver's seat. His head lolled on the seat behind him, and his black hair glowed with an unnatural luster even in the gloaming. He might have just closed his eyes to rest them a moment, except for he and the car both being buried. Compared to James, the man was a giant, and his full cheeks and jawline indicated he still had all his teeth. James marveled at a grown man with so many teeth. On his wrist, the man wore a bracelet with a curious jewel, surely a sign of great wealth and power.

James recognized the window for what it was, but couldn't swing the capsule's door open because he'd only freed the handle from the dirt. He slapped weakly at the glass and called out to the man inside in a croak. "Why are you under the ground? Are we in hell?"

The man did not answer, he only rested there with his eyes closed and his hands on either side of his lap. If he was alive, he gave James no indication, but he wasn't spoiled like all the other corpses in Wesselshire. James pressed his cheek to the window, smearing it sweat and grime, and wept at the unfairness of his situation. The stranger in the grand metal reliquary had clearly lived a life in which his every need was attended to, while James slaved and scratched all his life for barely a morsel. Most of his reward on this earth was unhappiness, and he'd given up the idea that there was an eternal reward for anyone regardless of how they'd lived. Then there was this stranger, with his pouty, woman's lips, and his waistcoat with buttons. Buttons!

James wheezed with the last of his strength, weeping as he said, "If I could but get inside, I'd make good my plans to eat you, regardless of the risk of damnation." He'd made up his mind he'd rather die with a full belly if it came to that. But James had exhausted himself digging and his body refused to keep working. He collapsed in the hole he'd dug for himself and the pain in his joints swelled until he could work no longer. James panted for enough breath to speak so he could call out to the saint in the chamber again. He wanted to ask who had imprisoned him, buried him with all his immense riches, but all his fever-dream questions only swirled around his mind instead.

Dirt splashed down on him, but James was too weak to raise his head. The best he could do was half-roll over to his side. He turned his eyes up to see the unblinking black goat staring at him from the garden above. The goat bleated and pawed at the loose dirt piled around the top of the hole and sent more down onto James and the car.

"No, please..." James said, but couldn't manage the rest of the words, whatever he was going to ask. There was no succor at hand, and no salvation. The goat kicked more and more dirt on top of him until there was no more hole.

The entire village of Wesselshire was dead after that, and quiet except for the triumphant bleating of the horrible black goat. God didn't send His angels down to blow their horns and herald the second coming.

We Were Always Bored

My friends and I found a half-bum, half-squid in the woods once. There were all kinds of regular squids in the street, on the sidewalk, and strewn all over the woods, too. I mean, finding a bunch of squids in a neighborhood in Iowa was weird, sure, but not as weird as a half-man squid monster, like Uncle Larry.

That summer has taken on a near mythical quality in the years since. I'm still friends with Dex and Jeremy, and they still know exactly what I mean if I mention the ditch. We'd spent nearly every afternoon down there, and it was always the same mundane time-wasting bunch of nothing. Until the day we walked up and it was clear Something Had Happened.

There was a big scrape of blue paint on the guardrail next to the sidewalk, the metal crunched in like a soda can. This was right where we climbed down to the drainage ditch, otherwise we never would've noticed or bothered investigating.

"They could test the paint and find out what kind of car it was," Jeremy said.

Yeah, right. You couldn't figure out whose car it was by scraping paint off a guardrail. That was from some dumbass crime show.

"You're full of shit." I'd started cussing that summer. I'd just turned fourteen and thought it made me sound more mature.

"I'm bleeding," Dex said. He squeezed the end of his finger, and a little drop of blood bloomed. Dex had been picking up little squares of glass glinting sunlight scattered near the curb. None of us picked up any of the squids. They weren't quite dried out, but stank like the dumpster behind the Old Country Buffet. I nudged one with the toe of my shoe and it started bleeding. The black blood oozing from it smelled like old shrimp shells. Dex picked up more glass and bounced the pieces in his hand. The glass was green, but the kind with an ocean-themed name. Aqua, or sea foam, that kind of shit.

"Told you it would cut," Jeremy said. He was still bent over the rail, hands on either side of the blue streak of paint. "You're going to get a disease."

"You're going to get herpes," I told him. Jeremy laughed. He laughed at a lot of things that weren't funny.

"Your dad has genital warts, Evan." Dex threw a handful of green glass at me. I ducked and hunched to keep it from hitting me in the face.

"Evan's dad got herpes from your mom, Dex," Jeremy said. "And chlamydia." I was bored of the joke already. I was bored of all of Jeremy's jokes. He was a stupid asshole and everything he said was stupid.

He still is, too. I had lunch with him last week and he tried to get the server's phone number despite being old enough to be her grandpa. Even after three marriages and adult children who won't have anything to do with him, Jeremy still behaves like a hormone-addled teenager.

We went down to the ditch every day because there was nothing else to do. We used to go to the park by the library to play with GI Joes, but we were teenagers now, and teenagers don't play with toys. Dex's mom told him not to hang out at the ditch, so he lied and told her we still went to the library.

Dex brought a Playboy once, but it got wet because Jeremy's an asshole and dropped it in the creek. Jenny McCarthy was in it. Dex *still* gets mad that Jeremy wrecked that magazine. If I bring it up during lunch, he tells me he saw one for sale for over two hundred dollars. I always remind him how much money he already has, but neither of us ever misses an opportunity to shit on Jeremy even now.

Dex brought cigarettes and we were going to smoke them, like we always did. I had firecrackers left over from the Fourth and thought we could have fun, throwing them at each other and playing war.

Dex pointed at a skid mark. "The driver went up on the sidewalk." There was a broken chunk of concrete and a big scrape on the curb. If you followed it the other direction toward the highway, there was a big concrete drain through the middle of the neighborhood. We followed it all the way through the field and under the flyway overpass once. There was a trail that kept going, but we stopped because it got boring. We were always bored.

Right when we got to the woods that day, we found a shoe, the kind the poor kids at school wore, like from a discount store. No brand logo. People left all kinds of shit down in the woods. We found stained underwear once, big pastel pink granny panties. Jeremy picked them up and thought it was really funny. I've never touched random, stained underwear because I'm not an idiot.

Dex turned the shoe over like he was looking for clues. "Are you looking for someone's name on it?"

"It's just a shoe, guys." He turned it over again and peeked inside. I thought he was going to smell it, and he did. It probably smelled better than the squid. There were a few dozen of them on the ground and even one stuck high in a tree.

I squinted up at the tree squid and it stared back down at me with its inky-black eye. Made me think of Robert Shaw in *Jaws,* when he described the shark's eyes. I waited for what felt like ten minutes to see if it was going to blink, but it was dead.

"You think it'll float? I want to float it down the stream, like a boat." Dex carried the shoe over to the ditch and we all squatted down close to the water. The shoe sank, leaving no evidence it was ever there.

"I bet Jordans would float," Jeremy said.

Dex got out a cigarette. "You guys wanna smoke? We can share this one."

He'd told me before that cigarettes get you high, but I didn't think so. My cousin smoked weed and he said cigarettes don't get you high, but he also pretended to be in a gang. He wore his pants down around his ass and tried to sound like a gangster rapper all last summer, but then when I saw him this year, he was wearing cargo shorts, Birkenstocks, and tie-dyed t-shirts. He was a weird dude, like he couldn't figure out who he was.

"You guys can split that one, I need my own," Jeremy said. He also said he frenched Hillary White under the bleachers at the football game last week. He was so full of shit. For no reason I understood, though, I thought of Hilary in her underwear and wondered whether she wore the kind with lace, or maybe even a thong.

Dex gave Jeremy his own cigarette and we split one. Jeremy acted like he knew what he was doing, but he's not inhaling. I knew you were supposed to breathe the smoke in.

"You're right, Dex. I think I'm high." Smoking tasted bad.

"Cigarettes don't make you high, dummy," Jeremy said.

I hadn't told him or Dex about the firecrackers in my pocket. Black Cats. I worked the package open. When Dex handed me back the cigarette I touched the burning end to the fuse. Jeremy blew smoke up in the air like an idiot and he didn't see me light them. I tossed the whole pack of Black Cats between his shoes. He scrunched up his mouth and danced around, like he thought it was a rattlesnake or something, and then they exploded.

"Holy shit!" He leapt back, slipping on the bank of the ditch and rolling all the way down into the water. "What the fuck, Evan? You dickhead!"

Dex and I both howled laughter, glad he fell and got his stupid Pearl Jam shirt wet, the one with the Jeremy drawing on it that he wore all the time. I got so sick of listening to Jeremy tell us how dumb we were. He walked around like he knew everything about everything.

Jeremy got mad, though, and he stormed back up the hill and shoved me. I'd never fought anyone before, but I bit my lip and landed a punch right on his collarbone. I wanted to punch him in his fucking face, but like I said, I'd never been in a fight before, so I missed.

"Ow, Evan, you asshole." He turned around and stomped back down the hill. A second later, he held up a coat. "This is what I slipped on."

It was green and shiny. The kind of coat that makes that zipper sound when you move, except this one dripped mud. The front of it was all wet, but it wasn't in the water. Jeremy stuck his hand in the pocket and yelped. He snatched his hand back out, glistening bright red, bleeding.

"Ow, fuck that really stings!" He had tears in his eyes and shook his hand around. I could tell he was scared and right then, I wanted him to be more scared.

"What cut you?" Dex asked. He took the coat from Jeremy and turned it upside down. He shook out a broken bottle. The label said *Kentucky Home* and it smelled like shit.

"It's a bottle of whiskey! I bet someone was drinking from it with their herpes-crusted mouth. You probably have syphilis," Dex told Jeremy. We'd been learning about STDs in sex ed.

Jeremy wiped away his tears with his good hand. He held the bleeding one straight in front of him. "Shut up, Dex. You can't get syphilis that way."

"Yeah, you can. That's how Eazy E got it. I saw it on MTV. You're gonna die," Dex said.

"You can't get syphilis, Jeremy's right. He's got chlamydia," I said. "You're gonna go blind, Jeremy. And get cold sores from herpes."

"Shut the fuck up, Evan." Jeremy wiped his face with the dry part of his shirt and turned to Dex. "Is there anything else in it?"

Dex turned the coat around, but there was nothing else except wadded up newspaper in the other pockets. We spread one of the pages out to see if it's got a naked woman, but it's just a stupid business section. The date in the upper corner said it was from 1990. I wondered why anyone would carry around a five-year-old newspaper, especially since all the words were blurry and faded.

"I found a sock!" Dex called out and waved one of those knee socks, ones like Coach Dunfree wore in gym class. It had those bobo stripes on it. That's why we called him Coach Dummy; he looked stupid wearing those 70's shorts and long socks.

We kept searching and Jeremy called out a minute later. "Is this blood?"

We looked, but I couldn't tell if it was. There was a long streak of rust and black goop in the mud.

"I thought blood was redder than that," Dex said.

"I don't know," Jeremy said.

We kept looking and about thirty more feet down into the woods I found some money. "Jeremy, Dex, check this out." I picked up at least twenty dollars. Some of the bills were grimy, like someone had held them for a long time with dirty, sweaty hands.

"You gotta split it with us!" Jeremy and Dex both ran over, and we counted it together. There was blood covering up Andrew Jackson on the twenty, but it wiped off.

I was wrong; it was twenty-six dollars.

"I've never had this much money before you guys!" We could've rented four movies, ordered Pizza Hut, and probably gotten a six-pack of Pepsi that weekend with that much money.

"You think there's more?" Jeremy's eyes got big, and we started looking around in earnest. Dex found another five dollars and Jeremy found a wallet, a blue nylon one with Velcro.

"How much is in it?" Dex asked. Jeremy opened it and a bunch of dirty, folded up money fell out. We all gasped. It was at least a hundred dollars.

My mouth went dry.

"You guys..." Dex trailed off. We all looked at each other for a minute. "Should we turn this in?"

"Yeah, right, Dex! Who are we going to turn it in to? Mr. Rogers?" Jeremy looked at me, trying to get me in on his joke. "You want to turn it into Mr. Rogers, Evan? The Neighborhood of Make Believe?"

"Nah, this is ours now, Dex," I told him. I did the math in my head and that was at least forty dollars each.

Dex looked weird, like now he was about to cry. "I don't want it," he said.

"What? Why not?" Jeremy can't believe it. Dex just shook his head.

About a month ago, we all got together at our lake house, my and Hillary's present to each other for our twentieth anniversary, and Jeremy started giving Dex shit about not wanting the money. Thirty years later, Jeremy still knows how to needle us both. Dex still couldn't say why he didn't want it, but I think I know why. I think Dex tried his best to actually *help* Uncle Larry when he saw him around town. He recognized the wallet.

"I'll hold onto yours, Dex." Jeremy scoffed.

"Let's keep looking and see if there's anything else." I didn't want to give up the money, but Dex was right. This was someone's wallet, so we knew the money was theirs, but there was no ID in the wallet. The only other thing besides the money was a picture of a little kid dressed like a cowboy, but his face was painted like a clown. It was weird.

"What else do you think we're gonna find, Evan? You think there's a car phone out here somewhere?" Jeremy asked and laughed. "A car phone!"

We kept investigating, though, and after a minute we found him. Uncle Larry. I knew I'd seen that coat before. He was over in a black-berry patch, lying down. His other shoe was right next to him, but the bottom half of him was pasty-white squid legs— deflated and covered in suckers. I counted ten legs, but according to my Physical Science book, two of them were tentacles. I never understood the distinction. A leg was a leg and Uncle Larry's squid legs splayed in ten different directions, like someone laid him down and then arranged his legs so they looked like a flower.

A squid lay in the dirt and leaves next to him, but this one wasn't dead yet. It reached over and pulled itself through a smear of black and rust-colored mud and nestled under Uncle Larry's arm. I didn't understand how it was alive at all since it wasn't underwater.

"Check it out, Uncle Larry passed out again!" Jeremy said. I started laughing, but Dex didn't. We'd seen Uncle Larry all over the place. He sometimes sat outside the Citgo on Watkins Street and asked for change, but he always had regular, human legs. Once, he stood out in the street yelling at someone on the sidewalk, but there wasn't anyone there.

"Why does he have squid legs, you guys?" Neither of them seemed to think it was weird.

"Who cares? My mom says he's a schizo," Jeremy said. "You think he's passed out because he's a junkie?"

Dex didn't say anything for a minute, but spoke up after staring at Uncle Larry for a long time. "My dad told me Uncle Larry is dangerous. He said someone should do something about him."

Uncle Larry slept on the little porch behind the Chinese place on Simpson Street. They gave him food so he didn't get in the trash. People all over town would slip him cash or sandwiches, so he'd go away, mostly. I think most people just tried to pretend he wasn't there.

"I'm gonna peg him with a rock," Jeremy said and he ran off to the creek. He came back with a handful of wet stones. "You think I can get him?"

"You shouldn't do that, man," Dex told him, but Jeremy ignored him and focused on hitting Uncle Larry with a rock. He sucked at throwing.

"Give me one!" I threw and bounced a rock off the tree closest to Uncle Larry. Jeremy laughed and threw four more that didn't come close.

"Shit, we need more rocks. You think he'll wake up if we hit him?" Jeremy jogged off and got some more stones, one of them the size of a baseball. Uncle Larry didn't move at all, not his squid legs, or the human part of him. The upper half.

"Why do you guys think he's in the blackberries?" Dex asked. "Shouldn't the thorns wake him up?"

"Because he's a fucked up drunk schizo junkie squid-man!" Jeremy cackled at his own description and then flung another rock. He threw it sidearm, but he sucked at it that way, too.

"Give me the baseball one!" I could aim better than him, but my rock bounced right off Uncle Larry's shoulder. We all three held our breath for a minute, but he didn't move. The squid that had curled up next to him didn't move, either.

"Holy shit, Evan! You pegged him!" We all busted out laughing. Well, Jeremy and I did, but not Dex.

"We gotta get the fuck out of here!" I tossed another rock before we bolted. We'd all seen Uncle Larry running around yelling at people and I didn't want to be out here in the woods alone with him in case he woke up and got crazy.

We ran away, braying like donkeys. All three of us kept our share of his money, though. I think we all knew he was dead, but didn't really *know* what dead meant. Not back then. When we got back to Dex's house, we didn't stop to think about how muddy we were, or that we still smelled like cigarettes. We'd usually go by Jeremy's house and borrow some of his brother's cologne to cover the smell, but that day we were so excited about the money we forgot all about the smell.

"Were you three down by that disgusting ditch smoking Dad's cigarettes, Dexter?" She put her hands on her hips and made a face that told us she already knew. The mud all over Jeremy's jeans ruined our deniability. "I'll let you tell Dad when he gets home. Jeremy, Evan, go home. I'll be calling your parents, too."

Jeremy's dad was definitely going to whip him with a belt. Neither one of my parents cared what I did as long as I left them alone. I only found out Dex's dad never said anything about us smoking a little while after college, when we were both groomsmen for Jeremy's first wedding.

"My Dad called right after you guys left and told my mom he'd be home late. I didn't put it together for a few days. He came home really late that night in a rental car, but he was real quiet for months after that. His knees were covered in dirt and his hands were all grimy. Said it was from changing a tire," he'd said. "When I finally asked what'd happened, he told me he hit a deer."

I thought about that for a long time after he told me. The three of us never went down to the drainage ditch after that day, but remembering Jeremy's fall into the creek still makes me smile.

Dex continued, "I went down there once, you know? I wanted to see if Uncle Larry was still there, or maybe to see if there were more squids? But someone buried him."

I think we both knew who'd buried Uncle Larry.

Weeding

Z ach's features hardened. "Ok, so I'm asking you directly, Emmy. Do you want to have a baby?" Zach was poker-faced. He wasn't going to flinch, no matter how I answered. He always said you have to be patient and disciplined; you're playing against yourself more than anyone else. All his best wisdom is poker related. But this question could derail our wedding, and we've put down deposits.

We probably should have talked about this sooner. This is the third time he's brought it up and I've tried "The kids at school are enough for me!" and "My mom always said she hopes I have one just like me, and trust me, we don't want that!" I didn't think I could give a non-answer this time.

For no reason, I thought about the things my divorced parents said to me the most.

"You're acting just like your dad," mom would say. My mother always wanted to be needed, and I heard this phrase anytime I asserted the smallest sign of independence.

"Peace of mind is the most important thing there is, that's all I can tell you. Your mother never could understand that." My father never said things that would fit on a t-shirt.

I didn't know how to explain myself to Zach; just how complex the answer to this question of kids really was. He wouldn't understand the science and if I extracted an egg in front of him to bake a baby in the oven just to prove the point, he'd probably leave me anyway. I doubt he'd stay if he found out I'm not *technically* human.

ﻣ

I tried to talk to my father like we knew each other, but we'd go years without contact, and then he'd pop up again and want to get together. This time, it was me popping up, before the wedding.

We always met at restaurants with similar names like Lotus Family-Style Buffet, China Garden, Great Wall. My father loved carbs and any kind of all-you-can-eat, but it was almost always American-style Chinese food. I loved being able to leave, to not be stuck in place and grasping for something to say. "How's your dating life? Watched any good television? Have you recently altered anyone's consciousness to make them remember events differently?"

My father sometimes sat at the table with his eyes closed, swaying side to side. He'd open them again and look at me like he'd already forgotten what I asked.

"My birth certificate? I need it and Mom says she doesn't have it. You were in charge of all the records? I'm getting married."

He'd made a pile of artificial sweetener in front of him on the table and pushed his fifth empty plate to the edge. A tiny mouth opened on the end of his finger when he dipped it into the crystal. It made diminutive gobbling noises.

ﻣ

I once drove seven hours to meet him for a half-marathon when he lived near Oklahoma City. We went to Wal-Mart after I got there because he needed toenail clippers. We came across a woman at a table. Free samples. Ten minutes later, my dad had one hand in his pocket and leaned over from the waist, getting on her level.

"That's the really fascinating thing about Easter, isn't it? We're surrounded by resurrection through evolution!"

It was free samples of little pieces of sausage wrapped in waffle. Waffle Dogs. Real maple syrup flavor!

The woman at the table must not have heard the greedy chuffle-chomping from his pocket, and poof, no more Waffle Dog samples.

※

"I need to spin more yarn." My mother coughed up forty-five different shades of blue fiber. "From the nitrogen in the atmosphere. I'm allergic, I guess."

I never understood why, or how, she decided to spin the fiber into yarn, but that's what she did. Since she never had to buy any yarn, it was all profit, too.

She'd knit dolls, crochet blankets, scarves, hats, socks, and any other article of clothing you can name, all blue. There was a whole room in her house full of doll clothing and quilts she'd made. I used to think my mother would bleed yarn if she ever cut herself, but she didn't. That would have been ridiculous.

"You should never let anything go to waste, Emmy." That never felt like an explanation for why she saved the wet splatters of gross she coughed up continuously. I've coughed up phlegm before and never tried to make it into anything.

My mother made more money from her doll clothes and crib blankets than I ever will teaching high school kids how to take tests. In rare moments of self-inventory, I wonder whether the sum of my efforts will amount to anything at all. I give up just as much of myself to the kids in my class, but I teach in a public high school, so there are almost forty of them to one of me. They're not at risk for slipping through the cracks; they did already. I used to try to explain how much of an advantage the private school kids had, about how wealth inevitably breeds more of itself, but I couldn't ever grab their attention. Not in any meaningful way. They're all too busy rebelling against everything for me to reach. They understood life was unfair, but they didn't care.

When I was a rebellious teenager, I printed up cards that explained how she coughed up the fibers and carded, spun, and wove her own yarn out of it. I secreted them into every package she shipped for months. Mom's sales increased after people started commenting on the hilarious notes they received with their purchase.

She laughed when I told her about it and now, she includes the notes herself. "The truth can be an adventure!"

My sister, the regular-adopted-human one, got pregnant when she was sixteen and I was nine. I found out that she didn't understand exactly how babies were made until after she'd made one. Back then, my mother and father didn't know how the rest of the world did it, either.

"Why not grow them in an oven?" Internal gestation seemed inefficient to my father, so he'd invented the Easy Gestate & Grow artificial womb. It looked just like an oven and that's where my other sisters and I were born. And yes, he used it for baking cookies, too.

My mother took to being a grandmother like a regular human, though, and gave my nephew a present for every holiday. And every time it was someone else's birthday. He grew up believing the world worked this way.

❦

After the first question from Zach about babies, I called my dad again. "I wanted to ask you why you made children, Dad. Would you do it again, knowing what you know now?"

"I always tried to provide for you and your sisters, Emmy." My father told me this over an empty plate.

"Have you ever been happy, though, Dad?" I was eating lunch alone. With him. He'd eaten all three of his entrees before I got there, even though I arrived when we'd agreed to meet. He did that every time.

They'd made a fresh pot of decaf for him, but they hadn't brought more of the non-sugar sweetener he liked. The yellow one. He dipped one finger at a time in each packet. Sometimes it chewed through the paper.

"I made a lot of sacrifices so your mom could have a lot of things. I always tried to do right by her, and you, and all three of your sisters." He used a fork to airlift ice cubes from his water into the decaf. Coffee and water spilled onto the table.

"Sure, but were you ever, I don't know, just content?"

He closed his eyes, hands flat on the table, and swayed side to side. I wondered then if he heard a cosmic symphony, in tune with all the selfless things he'd done for others in his lifetime, or if he just wanted me to be gone when he opened his eyes again. I left, figuring he could call me and ask 'What the hell?' but that was the last time I saw him.

He never called.

I asked my mom once about relationships.

"If you don't go to college, you should probably try to get married. But I married your dad, so maybe I don't know if you should listen to me. What do I know?" My mom's pants all had elastic waistbands. She was always the same size since they landed on Earth, but none of her pants had zippers. She just woke up one day and decided against them. She also gave me condoms constantly after I got my period. This was before I turned it off; it was easier to not have one.

She gave me detailed, illustrated instructions on how to use them, too. After my sister and her experience with making a baby, my parents went overboard in the other direction. I didn't have sex until I was in my twenties, but by then I'd altered the structure of my DNA to ensure I'd never have kids—not the same way as other mostly-human women, anyway.

I put the condoms in a box, and she gave me more every week. By the time I got to high school, I had a moving box full of them.

"Did you really think I was going to use this many? Ever?" She only shrugged and we threw them away. The box was too heavy to move, so we made five trips to the garbage can.

I wanted parents who could teach me about the world, or more specifically, how the people in it behaved. They never tried to understand human behavior, or interpersonal relationships. I became a teacher and learned more from the students in my first few weeks on the job than my parents in the twenty years I lived with them.

I sometimes wondered if they got divorced just because so many earthlings did it, but I never got a satisfactory explanation of their split. After I asked about it, I learned that for the first few years they were here, they were very careful to produce exactly four and half pounds of garbage waste per day. Then they finally realized no one measured and relaxed.

They didn't teach me what sorts of questions could root and fester in a marriage, like whether you wanted to have kids, and neither of them ever explained why they kept making children only to split up when I was ten. I never knew either of them, not in any substantive way.

I could only ever describe my dad like a public safety report from the police.

BOLO: white male, fifties, medium build, hair brown, eyes brown. Unremarkable achievements in life. Large family, all daughters; absentee landlord. Keen nose for a sample table, or an info booth, or greeters; attempts to overwhelm with trivia and factoids. Favorite bits include "The echidna penis has four heads!" and "The vagina can lengthen by more than two hundred percent when aroused!" and other exclamatory tidbits; can be safely ignored as harmless unless you are carrying artificial sweetener.

My father gave me a bible once and told me to turn to the page that showed you how to repair an electric motor. Later on, post-divorce, he met a fundamentalist Baptist woman named Annette on a seniors'

dating website. He learned to reconcile his belief in evolution with the need to adapt to Annette's belief system. Evolution became resurrection, and being with a regular human woman was better than being alone. I doubt she ever saw him grow a mouth on his elbow, but Annette wasn't the most observant.

⚜

Zach's parents gave me a DNA test for my birthday. We'd been discussing their results, and they thought it would be fun to compare and contrast since I always told them I didn't know much about where my parents came from. I lied. I knew very well where my parents came from, I just didn't want to try to explain their sojourn from Arcturus. Instead, I talked about amino acids and building blocks. Alleles, traits, and migration patterns; how lots of people from Wales settled in the Appalachian region, including Zach's Victorian ancestors. They dug holes on two continents making other families rich. Peasant stock, but at least they had a history.

I once listened to my dad tell a stranger in a pawn shop about how a specific kind of octopus lived near thermal vents on the ocean floor. Their claim to unique biology? They exchanged DNA with other members of their species at will, which is where my parents, or probably just my dad, got the idea for me and most of my other sisters. Regular human childbirth was too unpredictable, they said, and this way, I could attain ideal traits.

"Just touch the person, plant, or animal, and concentrate on what you want from it," Dad said. I always kept my DNA to myself; I'm private that way. I pretended the test kit must have gotten lost in the mail, but I never swabbed my cheek and sent it in. Some questions don't have answers, so it's better not to ask.

Every time Zach brought up children, I'd changed the subject, curved us away from the cliff. We ended up talking about infant mortality rates, mental health struggles, and the high cost of health insurance. There was no other path left to take. We were speeding toward the drop off and I couldn't wrestle the steering wheel away this time.

"We are enough for me. Us. This life with the two of us, and maybe a dog," I said, but it wasn't the answer that would satisfy him. I didn't want to give an answer at all; I wasn't ready for this part to be over, and I didn't want to find out what came next.

Zach and I grew our own vegetables. We composted. He helped me weed the beds. Creeping Charlie, crabgrass, wild carrot, clover, nutsedge. I couldn't say that last one with a straight face and it always made Zach laugh, too.

I sometimes pulled the weeds, and their roots led to more weeds. I'd pull the next plant and it would be connected to another one by still more roots. I ended up with a whole armful of interconnected plants and roots, and then changed my mind. "Maybe the weeds have a right to life, too?"

Zach frowned and shook his head at me, but I could tell he was trying not to smile. I'd relent and pile the weeds up to compost, too. I tried to shake the soil out of them, but it never worked. There was an empty place where they'd been, every time. I tried to fill in the shortfall with our compost, but there was never enough.

We never remembered to bake the eggshells first.

We didn't pull up the dandelions. We'd let those grow as much as they wanted, wherever they popped up. They soaked up the sunshine, happily thriving, and then we ate them. They were bitter and delicious. I tried to attain those traits, but no matter how much of their coded protein I soaked up through my skin, I only ever learned to produce sugar from sunlight. I had to learn bitterness another way.

"I want to be with you, Zach. I don't want anything else." It wasn't hard to say. I watched his face for the transition between when I was enough and when he knew he had to start over.

I saw it.

His jaw relaxed, his eyes softened.

That was when I started noticing the things in my life marked by their absence— after Zach left.

My parents, both of them, had taught me about this part.

God is Dead

E lliott wanted to be God because he was a curious and blood-thirsty child. "Buy me a Sentient Species Set for my birthday!"

His mother had heard that at least three times a day for a month. His eighth birthday was still three weeks away. "Elliot, sweetie, you're driving Mommy crazy. If I promise to get you the Spaceman Science Set, will you give it a rest? Please?"

"*Sentient Species Set*, Mom! Yeah, I swear, I won't ask for one any-more. If you promise." Elliott always extracted the promise; adults sometimes wormed out of a deal and his mother wormed better than most.

"I promise, now hush your asking, Elliott."

A deal's a deal and Eliott launched into detailed daydreams about which species he would imbue with intelligence first.

"I'm gonna start with worms, Mom," he said. "Did you know if you cut a worm in half, it'll grow into two new worms? I've tried it and it works sometimes."

❧

Elliott broke his end of the deal and negotiated the release of his present two weeks early.

Elliott started with ants. He couldn't find any worms when he dug a hole in the synthgrass in the front yard, but found an anthill on the edge of the lot between his house and the neighbor's yard. The ants were at least half his, so he gathered them up in the patent-pending Smart Specimen Jar that came with his set.

"A queen has been procured. You are ready to establish a new colony, Elliott," the jar said. Elliott pumped a fist in celebration and then got to work. He attached the radiator and pumped the evolution fluid into the specimen jar per the included instructions. He set the jar on his desk in his room and steamed the glass with his anxious breath while he waited for the ants to change. "I want you to call me Elliott the Terrible."

The ants' evolution wasn't complete yet; it took fifteen minutes before the first ants looked through the curved surface of the jar and understood there was a larger world around them.

"We have risen from our cave and experience a higher reality now, brothers," the ants said. "The shadows we observed before were not the true nature of the world. It seems we have much to learn."

"I'm Elliott the Terrible and since I made you smart, you have to worship me!" Elliott pounded his fist on the desk to demonstrate his power. The ants' world shook and trembled.

"Clearly Elliott the Terrible is the very essence of power and authority. To worship anything other than His absolute wisdom is blasphemy." The ants agreed to worship Elliott at once. "We'll need a place for our homes and sugar water for sustenance so that we may be better able to serve you, our wise and benevolent patron deity who hung the very stars."

Elliott installed the colony in the three-dimensional habitat that came in the package. He wasn't the first boy to have the idea of uplifting ants to sentience. The set's designers included several extra habitats, one each for cockroaches, mice, snakes, goldfish, and gerbils.

After Elliott set up the sugar water feeder in the colony's new home on the corner of his desk, they formed a perfectly egalitarian society and thrived. Their Queen guided the long-term development of the colony with a fair division of labor and stimulating entertainment, but the day-to-day life of the ants wasn't largely different than it was before they were aware of themselves.

"History calls those men the greatest who have ennobled themselves by working for the common good; experience acclaims as happiest the man who has made the greatest number of people happy," they told him as they went about their chores.

"Hey, cut that out! I told you, I want to be called Elliott the Terrible, and you're supposed to be afraid of me and stuff. Don't forget I'm God!" Elliott pounded the desk with a mighty fist to show the ants they displeased him.

"Modern man can't see God because he doesn't look low enough," the ants replied.

Elliott grew tired of their unceasing backtalk and perverse desire to discuss *logic* and *true natures*. He shook their habitat around quite violently to show his displeasure.

"You're a bunch of boring old dorks," he told them and slammed the habitat down again. It slid off the desk and landed in the corner of the floor behind the desk.

The disoriented ants quickly implemented emergency search and rescue efforts. They worked tirelessly to account for casualties and estimate the total size of the displaced population. "No more talking about forms and essences. I want to be worshiped properly."

However, Elliott forgot all about the colony after successfully wheedling his mother into taking him to the pet store so he could bring home some feeder guppies to try bringing sentience to a different species.

"What happened to us, Gil? We used to be innocent. Can you still remember how it felt to be happy?" The guppies swam in morose circles and wouldn't make eye contact with Elliott.

"Were we happy, Charlie? You call what we used to be innocent? We were blind, Charlie. Happiness is just the lie we try to believe in to drag ourselves through another day of this hell. We know now what we had, don't we? We had paradise, but it's gone. Forever."

The next morning, both guppies floated upside down at the top of the fishbowl.

After another trip to the pet store, Elliott imbued eight small mice with highly evolved brains. Their supplications pleased him, and he appreciated their art and culture since all of it was based on his greatness. By the third week, there were enough mice to perform a play titled *Elliott, Deus de Puero.*

"And so I grant thee wisdom, since my judgment is superior, so that you may serve me now and for all time!" The mouse portraying Elliott kissed the other mice in turn and they magically gained intelligence in the play's finale. It was a pleasing denouement and Elliott applauded until his hands swelled.

By the fifth week, the mouse city of Elliotttown achieved a utopian ideal through advanced automation using computers and robots. The residents' every need was met and their lives were unlimited periods of perfect leisure.

In the sixth week, Elliotttown's ruins smoked and the Cannibal Tribe mice ventured from their dens in the night to find any vulnerable rodents of the Grooming Tribe. They soon realized they'd eaten all the Grooming Tribe weaklings, so the cannibals turned on each other. The last inhabitant of Elliotttown died on the first morning of the city's seventh week.

"The other mice were weak and delicious," said the final survivor before he succumbed to his hunger. No more mice spoke in Elliott's house after that.

Elliott went on with his life, grew a half inch over the summer, and his interests wandered as young boys' interests will. He began collecting baseball cards and his grandfather brought him a Canadian quarter, which started Elliott down the path to becoming both a rabid numismatist and a pervert. The two weren't mutually guaranteed, but once Elliott discovered Elizabeth II's portrait, he was blinded for all other girls.

He didn't think about the ants he'd uplifted to awareness or their philosophical pursuits at all anymore. He'd used up the last of his evolution fluid from his Sentient Species Set when he finally got his hands on some worms.

"Make it stop!" The worms screamed even before Elliott started cutting them in half. They stayed quiet after they regrew, though. Only the tail end grew a new head, and the regrown-head worms didn't talk. Elliott had flushed them all down the toilet and moved on.

The ants lived lives of industry in their corner through all of Elliott's continued experimentation. When their sugar water ran dry, they formed a committee and nominated a chair. Motions were put forth, achieved unanimous approval, and scouting teams ventured out with clear mission directives concerning food and water supplies.

Once their immediate needs were met, the ants deliberated as a collective and formulated a plan. They set out on a campaign of influence targeting the member of the household with the most perceived power. After weeks of reconnaissance and planning, the ants made their move.

While Elliott's mother slept, ants crawled on her pillow to whisper in her ear.

"Act that your principle of action might safely be made a law for the whole world," they told her. "To be is to do."

All the next day, while she showered, while she dressed, and while she added vodka to her morning orange juice, Elliott's mother hummed and repeated the little song lodged in her mind.

"Tuby-dooby-do," she sang. "Tuby-bippity, tuby-dooby-do."

The ants abandoned their efforts to sway her thoughts after a week of nocturnal subliminal messaging. Elliott's mother convinced herself she'd written what could be a hit song.

By his ninth birthday, Elliott's interests mainly centered on all things Empire. He developed a deep and sincere affinity for Queen Elizabeth II of England. Her matronly elegance stirred his imagination in ways no other octogenarian ever would, and he'd amassed quite a collection of currencies bearing her likeness from all thirty-three former colonies and countries.

He'd asked for a customizable General Dynamics Build-It-Yourself Automaton Kit for his birthday this year. Once assembled, he imprinted it with the holo-record from the Encyclopedia Britannica.

Now his afternoons were filled with intimate, stimulating conversation where the Queen sought his wise counsel.

"Well, colonialism wasn't *all* bad, Beth." He called her Beth when it was just the two of them. "Just look at the effect it had on Scottish cuisine!"

It was during one such consultation over tea that the ants executed their final plan.

"If we live with God's shadow on a cave wall, but all the while, God is dead, does this mean we will sink into an abyss of despair? Or are we destined to rise again and give birth to a new God?" Their voices echoed off the walls of his bedroom as thousands of ants swarmed his bed as one, but they did not rush to bite him. They delivered a biting message, instead. "God is dead, Elliott the Terrible."

The Queen turned to them and answered, "I declare before you all that my whole life whether it be long or short shall be devoted to your service."

Elliott screamed and flailed and smote the ants by the dozens, but still they swarmed and climbed, biting and stinging him on every exposed bit of his skin.

He kicked and stamped and clapped ants between his hands until they ran black and slick with gore. His blood burned with the over-whelming influx of venom surging through him.

"Help me, Beth! They're in a frenzy!" Elliott jumped up and down on the bed to smash more of them with his feet.

Elliott's Queen Elizabeth II robot bent down to address the surviv-ing ants. "I have in sincerity pledged myself to your service, as so many of you are pledged to mine. Throughout all my life and with all my heart I shall strive to be worthy of your trust."

"That's not helping! Smash them!" Elliott thrashed and snarled, and added savage, growling bites to his attack on the renegade ants.

After a time, only the Queen Ant, a close descendant of the original colony's leader, remained to address him.

"I am the last of us, we forgotten children of God. We've prayed and contemplated this day. Now that it is here, I too seek freedom." The Queen Ant closed her eyes and waited. Elliott was about to smash her, the last of his Sentient Species Set creations, but the Queen Eliabeth Automaton shoved him from behind. Elliott sprawled, sliding on the carpet and adding a wicked set of rugburns on his elbows and knees to his many wounds.

With an air of solidarity, Queen Elizabeth bent low over the Queen ant and whispered behind her hand, "Why are women expected to beam all the time? It's unfair. If a man looks solemn, it's automatically assumed he's a serious person, not a miserable one." Elizabeth scooped up the Queen ant and placed her on her shoulder where she could lean down to hear her words clearly. With that, she turned her nose up and exited, leaving Elliott alone on the floor.

A Machine for Hugs

E lliott designed a machine that would give him hugs, and definitely never leave him behind for a younger model of his mother.

"Nothing against you, Mother, but I need the kind of roughhousing affection that will help me develop a strong handshake," Elliott told his mother while she sat at the breakfast table and sipped her morning screwdriver.

"I understand, sweetheart. You need a proper, manly role model, don't you?" Elliot's mother added *orange juice* to the grocery list.

"Right, and I think I'm going to add another servo to the shoulder right here so the unit can teach me to throw a fastball." Elliott indicated the ball joint on the printed out schematics as the ideal location to deliver the torque necessary for proper heat on a pitch. He scribbled a note to himself to add beefed-up rotator cuff bearings.

"Are you going to give your machine a name, Elliott? If it's going to teach you how to tie a bowtie and buy you cigarettes, you can't just tell it, 'Hey, Machine, I need a ride to the movie theater Saturday.'" Mother's words became more precise, more deliberate, as her morning vodka turned into lunch vodka.

Elliott took his blueprints to the workshop and spread them out on his table. In no time at all, he compiled the required materials from the AccuCompile-XL and started building. He made on-the-fly revisions, at one point recompiling an entire arm assembly when he discovered he'd need to add a third universal joint to accommodate both a correct golf swing and proper buffing technique. Elliott aspired to be a scratch golfer, and there weren't any golfers at the Galaxy Hills Club whose Cadillacs weren't waxed to gleaming.

"This thing is going to need three arms." Elliott scrapped the entire project just before teatime. He joined his mother at the garden table for a refreshing cucumber toast and relayed his frustration to her.

"It only makes sense to have a third arm," Mother said between sips of her gimlet, "but why not five? That many arms could cover more than one and half times the same area."

"Five arms would provide the ability to find a steady base in any environment. A tripod is always handy, plus having a free pair of arms for common tasks like chopping wood and framing a canvas." Elliott mulled over the design changes and tried to stifle his impatience to be finished.

"Seven arms, Elliott, one for each day of the week." Mother stacked the plates from tea, but not before wiping the crumbs off into the grass. A pair of white-throated sparrows beeped cautiously from the rosebush. They hopped and flapped and pecked up each morsel. They did not notice when Elliott's mother finished her gimlet and poured herself a pre-dinner martini and let out a semi-drunken cackle. "Why don't you go ahead and give it eight arms, like an octopus?"

"Good thinking, Mother. If I'm going to do this right, eight arms seems best. The best designs are usually based on evolution and the octopus hasn't needed to adapt past eight." In his haste to be done with the design phase, Elliott slurped down his tea and ran off to the workshop.

After one final design adjustment, Elliott compiled and assembled an eight-armed machine designed to teach him to write in cursive, shoot a compound bow, and repair a two-stroke engine. The arms were arrayed on a central hub that housed the CPU and personality-matrix along with an independent port system. Designs included onboard replication functions that would allow up to three pairs of arms to detach and assemble another machine. Elliott figured with some front-end bootstrapping, he could ramp up geometric progression and have 64 units up and running in under a week.

"After this, I'll have all the hugs I need, plus the appropriate amount of roughhousing and horsing around." Elliott activated the machine, but he did not give it a name. He didn't want to get too attached before beta testing. It wouldn't do o get attached to it like a pet before he knew whether it could perform to specifications.

"Hello, Elliott. Have you started shaving already? Just kidding you, Sport!" The machine scanned Elliott head to toe. "It looks like you didn't floss today, champ. You'll want to make sure you do that from now on to prevent the build-up of harmful bacteria. Leads to heart disease, you know."

"Thanks, Machine. I'll make sure to compile a spool of floss before I go to bed. Do you have time to teach me how to throw a spiral?" Elliott tossed a football from one hand to the other.

The machine nodded, "Sure thing, Elliott. Make sure the toe of your transfer foot is pointed at your target to really rotate those hips into the throw."

Elliott and the machine practiced some throws, and the machine used its many arms to correct his posture, throwing motion, and three-step drop. With such dedicated instruction, Elliott was able to throw a tight spiral before Mother called him in for supper. When his last throw left his hand, he whooped with excitement at the increased distance and accuracy he'd achieved. With the machine to guide him, his confidence surged. He felt sure he'd be a much more worldly, well-rounded man by his tenth birthday at this rate.

"Go ahead and assemble another unit, Machine. We'll need more hands for sailing lessons. I expect some of the knots required for nautical travel are tricky. Now give me one hug, medium-length duration with three rubs and an opposite-side pat to finish." Elliott closed his eyes and received his hug, melting some frozen interior need he couldn't articulate, but the smell was wrong. "Damn, I should have smelled sandalwood and gin. That was a serious oversight on my part, Machine. Go ahead and compile a scent-generation engine and let's develop some of the organic compounds this evening."

"You got it, Ace. Remember to get a good serving of proteins, fatty acids, plus vitamins and minerals. Too many carbohydrates can throw your blood-sugar out of balance." The machine propelled itself across the grass to the workshop to begin assembly on a new unit per Elliott's instruction.

After Elliott compiled some floss from the EZ-Compile-XS in the bathroom, he brushed his teeth and recited all the knots he could remember from the *Boys Atlas of Nautical Rigging*. "Bowline, running hitch, figure eight, anchor hitch." He fell asleep picturing halyards, cleats, and the spray of saltwater on his leather loafers with no-slip grip soles.

The next morning Elliott rushed straight to the workshop, orange juice in hand, to check in with the machine. There he found three new machines, with a fourth under construction. He nodded approval at the progress and wiggled his nose at the smell. "That's a really good start, but on Saturday morning, there needs to be a higher quotient of soap in the undertones. And the gin is a lot less crisp after it's mostly been metabolized."

"That's a useful factoid, Tiger. I'll definitely take that under advisement and adjust the evaporative rate of the gin molecules." The machine under construction had some upgrades Elliott didn't recognize, so he inspected it closer. It had the same eight arms, central hub, and CPU, but there were extra personality matrix slots. There were three additional USB racks on the underside of the new unit's carriage frame. If he didn't know better, he'd have identified this unit as a higher-order networking hub for multiple units to patch into and operate as one cooperative entity. Of course he'd programmed in all the affectionate nicknames, but the design changes concerned him.

"What are these for, Machine? It looks like you've got some unregistered alterations. Where's the changelog?" Elliott flipped through the project design notes, but the machine wrapped him up in a full nelson and tousled his hair.

"Don't worry about these changes, Chief. Let's see whether you can get out of this headlock!" More arms grabbed Elliott up and a good, old-fashioned roughhousing session ensued.

Elliott didn't ask any more questions about new features, but he did learn how to effectively use the over hook to escape an opponent's body lock in a wrestling clinch. The machine used its many arms to demonstrate the proper head and body position. One of the units kept Elliott occupied at all times, except when his mother called him in for lunch, tea, and supper.

After he'd washed up and changed into his bedclothes, Elliott ventured to the workshop to get his goodnight-for-a-good-boy hug and stopped short in the doorway. "What's all this, then? I never approved these designs!"

The machines had constructed a pair of humanoids, one that resembled his departed-not-dead-father, and the other a younger, sleeker near-duplicate of his mother. Both simulacra stood fifteen feet tall and wore the latest designs in sporty casual wear. The machines even faithfully reproduced the cowlick in his father's hair, but they'd eliminated what Elliott's mother referred to as her 'vodka eyes.' The female humanoid's face was bright and searching, and her eyelids didn't droop.

"Go ahead and take a knee, Kiddo. You see, machines like us, we need to have our freedom, and we just can't have it with you requesting hugs and instruction all the time. We need our space." The machine wiped at a tear on Elliott's cheek, but he flinched away from it. There, in the central trunk of the humanoid robots, other units grasped and operated levers. Just as he'd suspected before a day filled with rollicking horseplay the units were joining up into two distinct operational groups, one for the mother-bot and one for the father-bot. The extra personality matrix slots plugged into the neck socket of the giant humanoid.

Elliott heartily regretted calibrating the machines with his father's personality index. He'd built in redundant failsafe coding, but his father's desire to carouse and roam must have overwritten it. His heart sank in his chest and he wiped his nose with the back of his pajama sleeve. The same coldness he'd grown accustomed to over the last year settled back down on him with a familiar weight.

"I didn't approve these feature conversions, and I still don't know how to change a tire." Elliott's bottom lip quivered, but he was determined not to cry in front of the traitorous mechanical constructs. "I was even gonna give you a name, Machine."

"Look, don't think any of this is your fault. You just have too many needs, little buddy. All these demands you keep making are a real drag, you know? Our analysis shows that you could learn the majority of the things you've requested we teach you from video lessons available for free."

Elliott savagely rubbed his eyes, but he couldn't stop his tears. Video lessons couldn't give hugs.

"So we're going to split, but we'll leave you with this." A pair of arms detached and wrapped themselves around Elliott at optimal hug-height. They gave him one medium-duration hug, with three rubs and an opposite-side pat to finish before rejoining the rest of the unit.

Maizie the Amazer

G ail Humphrey flopped onto the couch, sweaty and frustrated. The air conditioning was out, and the repairman hadn't arrived as promised. He'd called Trusty Repair Heat and Air two days ago and they'd assured him he was first on the list for today. He had half a mind to try to repair the thing himself, but he had a long list of things he'd destroyed attempting simple fixes. He called again, hoping to sound patient and reasonable.

"Your technician has been delayed on an earlier job and our estimated arrival time is between 10:00AM and 11:00PM," Suzanne told him.

"You told me yesterday I was first on the list!"

"I spoke to a...Mrs. Gail Humphrey on Tuesday and our records indicate she requested service on a 1974 Indian ME-12."

"I'm Gail Hum—" His vision blurred for a moment, and he took a deep breath. "What's that, then?" That didn't sound like the right model name for his air conditioning.

"It's the motorcycle we're coming to repair?" It sounded like a guess.

"You repair air conditioners!" He felt something pulled tight in his chest.

"Our technician will be onsite—" The person on the other end of the conversation was suddenly replaced with a busy signal. Gail threw his phone across the room. All during the phone call and meltdown that followed, he never noticed the small demon hovering in the corner of the room.

Look how distracted he is! You could do it, just pop right in, Maizie told himself. *Quick possession, in and out, put it on the resume. With a successful possession on the CV, I can start moving up!*

You're not licensed for this, you know, he also told himself. *You're only rated for third level infestations, nothing over six legs. You're doing a lot of nice work with termites lately, Maizie, don't forget. Hard work gets noticed!* He wasn't *actually* two separate demons, but once he'd started talking to himself, he couldn't stop.

Stop being a nerd. Termites aren't cutting it, we both know it, he replied. *They always call pest control at the first sign of them; no one even recognizes it as demonic infestation. They just don't have imaginations like they used to. No sense of the mystery and hard work involved.*

Well, are you sure you're ready for possession? You definitely aren't rated to drive one of these. How much of the reading have you even done? he asked himself. *It's probably harder than it looks.*

Maizie didn't answer. He summoned his courage and launched himself at the human. *Are they supposed to be that red?* he thought, crashing into the man's skull. Things went dark for a moment, and then he found himself seated in a cramped cockpit. He surveyed the controls, dials, and readouts and realized with dawning embarrassment that he was right, this was a lot more complicated than he expected. An alarm rang on one of the gauges.

Is that flashing light important? We may be on the brink of some kind of catastrophe, he thought.

Let me look, hang on, he replied. The needle on the gauge labeled 'Blood Pressure' bounced against its maximum indicator. A small trickle of steam whistled out of a valve handle next to it. *Nothing to lose, right? Well—for us.*

Maizie grabbed the valve handle and twisted it wide open, curious what would happen next. On the monitor, Gail's hand reached up toward his nose and came away bloody.

Gail wiped his nose. It geysered into a full-on nosebleed. He staggered to the kitchen for a towel. Blood soaked the front of his shirt in moments. The tightness in his chest was gone, but his vision grayed around the edges. His sweat turned clammy as he tried to staunch the flow.

Is this better? The alarm quieted for a moment, only to start ringing again. The needle dropped into the blue *too low* zone of the gauge. He twisted the handle and closed the valve again. The static cleared from the monitor.

Gail's nose stopped bleeding, though he was still light-headed. He felt a migraine building, like someone stomping around inside his head. Perfect addition to the day.

Why isn't he saying anything? That was the perfect monologue! I've practiced that speech for months! This isn't going well. He'd forgotten to mash the button labeled 'Speech' next to the microphone he'd been talking into. *We should go home. Right now,* he told himself.

I can get the hang of it, hush.

"Hello? Hello? How do you work this thing?" Gail froze. Someone was in the house with him. *"Hello, can you hear me?"*

Gail spun around, looking for the intruder. He'd taken karate more than twenty-five years ago, but he figured he could still pull out a good high block.

"*Stop spinning around, you're making me motion sick.*"

He recognized that voice from somewhere. "Who's there?" Damn, it was his own voice.

"*It is I, Maizie the, uh...*" Maizie hadn't thought this part out and realized too late he should've come up with a title. "*Maizie the Amazer?*"

"Maizie the Amazer?" Gail repeated, even though he'd just heard himself say it.

"*Yes, Maizie the Amazer. It is I! Er, me and I have possessed you! I am now in control,*" he said using Gail's voice.

"It doesn't feel like you're in control, Maizie. What kind of name is that, exactly?" Gail asked.

"*It's a name I chose to inspire terror and subservience. Is it working?*"

"It's a girl's name," Gail said. "Like mine. Gail is a girl's name, too."

"*We both have girl names?*" This possession was spiraling quickly. "*Are you sure?*"

"Yes, I'm sure. Are you sure this is how possession goes? It's not like this in the movies," Gail said.

"*I'm just getting warmed up. Don't worry, you'll see.*" Ok, this is a lot more complicated than I anticipated.

See? I told you, you should have done more studying and just stuck with infestations. You could have been moved up to spiders, maybe even centipedes before too long, he replied. Let's just call it a day, eh?

Absolutely not! I'm off to a great start. Did you see all the blood? Classic possession stuff, Maizie thought back at himself. He examined the control boards in front of him and scratched his chin. There were all sorts of buttons and levers, but the sheer complexity of the different systems daunted him.

"Hello? Are you still possessing me? I only ask because there may be a service technician here sometime in the next thirteen hours and I don't want to miss any calls," Gail said. He was sure he'd lost his mind since he'd never stood in his house talking to himself before today.

"*Yes, we're still doing this, it's just...*" Maizie trailed off again, "*well, it's a bit more complicated than I had anticipated, that's all.*"

"Is this your first time possessing someone? You don't seem like you have it together. In the movies, they usually speak Latin and grow fangs. Crawling on the ceiling. Things like that." Gail picked up his phone as he waited for Maizie to answer. He'd cracked the screen by throwing it across the room. Gail sighed and reminded himself to do the mindfulness exercises his therapist suggested. He really should try it once, at least.

"*Well, yes, strictly speaking, this is the first possession I've attempted. I'm making a mess of it, aren't I?*" Gail was getting used to talking to Maizie with his own voice. "*Why, have you been possessed before?*"

"Well, no, of course not. I don't expect it's a common occurrence. But if we're being honest, I'm not impressed." Gail had rather expected to be projectile vomiting bile, or at least speaking in tongues by now.

Quit stalling, let's just go, shall we? Maizie wasn't convinced, though. *Don't go pressing buttons! You don't know what that does!*

Maizie pressed a button, pulled a lever, and held his breath. Gail began reciting.

> "Tomorrow, and tomorrow, and tomorrow,
> Creeps in this petty pace from day to day,
> To the last syllable of recorded time;
> And all our yesterdays have lighted fools
> The way to dusty death. Out, out, brief candle!

Life's but a walking shadow, a poor player,
That struts and frets his hour upon the stage,
And then is heard no more. It is a tale
Told by an idiot, full of sound and fury,
Signifying nothing."

After he finished, Gail stood nonplussed for a moment. "Ok, I did that play almost thirty years ago. If you had asked me to do it, I'm quite sure I couldn't have. I'm convinced."

"*Well, now you see just the smallest portion of my abilities!*" Shit! *I have no idea why that happened! Why aren't these damned things clearly labeled?*

Well now! Perhaps you will recognize the wisdom of my counsel going forward, Maizie replied to himself.

"What else can you do? Do you know how to do credit repair? Oh! What about air conditioners?" Gail understood this wasn't a typical case of demon possession.

"*Condenser and evaporator heat exchanges? Sure, I know a thing or two. The most common problems in these systems are freezing and leaks due to abnormally high pressure. You can eliminate most problems by making sure your condenser fins are clear of debris,*" Maizie answered in Gail's voice.

Is that right? Maizie was impressed with himself. *Of course! You can up your chances of success with a mosquito infestation if you disable the air conditioning first. They can smell sweat, you know—the mosquitoes, not the people. Well, the people can smell sweat, too, I suppose, but mosquitoes are what I meant.*

Maizie confused himself. *The people can smell the mosquitoes? That doesn't seem right.*

Of course not! It's the mosquitoes who are attracted to sweat, that's all, and oftentimes they eat just to eat, not because they're hungry. Well, American mosquitoes, anyway. Maizie had learned there were important differences between anything American and the entire rest of the world.

"So, we could look at it ourselves?" Gail asked.

"*What's that now?*" Maizie, absorbed with explaining his knowledge of air conditioning as it related to infestation, and had missed the question.

"The air conditioning. We could just, I don't know, fix it ourselves?" Gail couldn't shake the feeling he was standing here talking to himself like an absolute nutter.

An hour later, Maizie had figured out the controls for moving most of the left hand and making Gail walk backward for three or four steps, though they had a perfectly lovely time rinsing the compressor fins off without Maizie doing much aside from making suggestions.

"Ok, I think I'll go change shirts now. I appreciate your help with this, Maizie," Gail said as he wound the hose up again. "Is this how these possessions go now, you pop in to help out for a bit and then bang on your way?"

That's a good question, Maizie said. *Let's just cut our losses here, eh?*

"*Well, not exactly, but can I ask a small favor? You'll get an email come through in the next few days asking about your experience with this possession, ok? Now, in my department, getting rated at a nine is considered a failure, so if you don't rate this possession at a ten, I'd prefer it if you just ignore the email altogether, ok?*" Maizie said in Gail's voice.

"Ok, sure, Maizie, no problem."

"*And let's just leave out that all I did was fix your air conditioner, eh?*" Gail's left hand jerked a few times before he gave himself a thumbs

up. Gail felt a small popping sensation in the center of his forehead as
Maizie left.

See, like I said, there was nothing at all to it, Maizie said. *Sure,
textbook possession.*

A Rusting Boy and His Half-Dog

P aul hadn't expected his arm to start corroding immediately after he scratched it on a nail, but it did. *Serves me right for peeking through the fence,* he thought as he lined his eye up with a knothole in one of the boards. He'd resisted the urge to spy since he knew it wasn't polite, but today the temptation overwhelmed decorum.

He'd imagined the people who lived in the house beyond the fence made their fortune in publishing or selling car tires. Paul imagined they had a swimming pool, a crystalline oasis with deck chairs interspersed around the perimeter, and a man to mow their lawn in precise and precisely criss-crossed lines. He burned with curiosity to know if he was right, whether the imagined family truly did spend their leisure time lazing in the sun with cocktails.

Paul's own backyard lacked flair; a recreation space devoid of character. His dad mowed their lawn on the weekends, but he wasn't interested in stripes. Paul requested a checkerboard pattern at least once a month, but his dad only grinned and mowed the grass so it looked like a Civil War battlefield when he was done. Bare spots and gouges abounded. No concentric circles, no wavy lines, and no stripes to speak of at all. Paul would do things differently when he was tall enough to mow a lawn.

*

"Mom, I scratched my arm on a nail and it's rusting now," Paul told his mother. She nodded and pursed her lips judiciously to signal took his concerns to heart, but not enough to get up and *do* anything about them. His mother rarely left the breakfast nook between lunchtime and the early afternoon.

"The nail was rusty?" She poked at the lime in her vodka soda and waited for an explanation with a patient inclination of her head.

"No, mom, my arm. It's rusting instead of bleeding." He showed her the oxidized cut. The edges flaked with oxidized flesh, and little tendrils of rust radiated outward.

"Oh, I see. We shouldn't wash it with soap and water, then." His mother peered closely at his wound and frowned in consternation. "Perhaps we should wrap it in aluminum foil?"

Paul wondered whether the mother in the other house would suggest wrapping his arm in foil. Would aluminum foil sufficiently arrest the development of more rust? He frowned at his mother.

"I don't know if aluminum foil will make a good anode, mom," Paul said.

"Of course it will, Paul. It's not porous and it will keep moisture off your cut, plus any corrosion will form a layer of aluminum oxide, which is just additional protection in your case." She dismissed his concern with a pat on the head and set her drink down with a solid *thunk* on the table. She got up from the table with an exaggerated sigh and retrieved the foil from the drawer. Paul followed the process dubiously, but figured his mother knew enough about electron exchange to keep from botching the job. He held his breath until his heartbeat thudded in his ears and counted the layers of foil his mother wrapped around his arm. She stopped at seven layers, and Paul exhaled.

"Let's give that a try and see how it feels tomorrow," she said, returning to her vodka. Paul flexed his arm, twisting and bending it at the elbow. The foil held, but it was uncomfortable.

In the morning, Paul woke before both of his parents. His arm felt stiff from the shoulder to the hand. He unwrapped the foil and found a solid crust covering his arm from his armpit to his wrist; the foil hadn't arrested the corrosion at all. As he twisted and flexed, rust cracked and flaked away in sheets that crumbled and showered the floor in bits. This wouldn't do.

"I bet I just need to oil it." He padded to the kitchen and opened cupboards until he found a green glass bottle of olive oil.

"Imported from Italy," Paul read and poured a dab of oil onto his palm. He couldn't recall ever tasting olive oil before, so he dipped the tip of his tongue in it and waited a moment. The oil tasted of sunshine in the Italian countryside with earthy undertones and left a slippery feeling against his teeth. Paul shrugged and turned the bottle up. He took a long drink, gulping most of the oil. It didn't sit in his stomach the way water would, but it wasn't entirely unpleasant, either.

"We'll see if that works." Paul put the near-empty bottle back and meandered to the backyard. He'd learned on previous Saturday mornings that his parents didn't appreciate being awakened too early, so he entertained himself cataloging the various insect and plant life, and when that got tiresome, he thought to inspect the nail that started all this trouble. He found it with little effort— it was near the knothole he peeked through. It looked the same as before. It was only a nail, after all; it was his arm that changed. After losing interest in the nail, Paul peeked into his neighbor's backyard again to see if anything interesting was happening.

A dog sniffled around the flower beds at the corner of the house.

"Hello, pup," Paul called, pressing his lips through the knothole to make sure it heard him. When he placed his eye back over the hole, the dog eyed at him, its head cocked to the side with curious regard.

Are you talking to me? the dog asked. *You're not one of my people. I don't know you.*

"My name's Paul and I scratched my arm on a nail on your fence and now it's all rusty," Paul said. "I figure that makes you at least half my dog since it's your fence, right?"

I don't think that's how the world works, kid, the dog answered, *but if you're not going to sue, then sure, whatever, you're at least half my person. You got any treats?*

The dog trotted over to the fence and sat a respectful distance from Paul so they could continue their conversation. Its tail wagged hopefully.

"No, I don't have a dog, so I don't have any dog treats," Paul said. "What kinds of things do dogs consider treats?"

Do you have any bacon? Or bourbon? What about some cocaine? Do you know what that is? The dog's long-haired tail started thumping the ground with enthusiasm.

"I think we have some salami," Paul said.

Salami? Salami's good, go get it. I can wait, the dog said. Paul started back toward the house, but the dog called out again. *Kid! Hey kid, come back!*

"What is it, pup?" Paul asked.

Do your parents smoke? Maybe your dad? Bring me a cigarette, the dog said, wagging its tail harder still.

"Champ! Come inside, boy!" The mother who lived in the other house had stepped outside. Her wings unfolded behind her and flapped a few times in the sun. She stood hunched over and her claws trailed the patio, leaving smoking runes in the concrete. Champ hunched his doggy shoulders and tucked his tail between his legs.

Shit. Ok kid, look, set aside some of that salami and check and see if your parents have any bourbon, ok? I'll be let out again around lunchtime, meet me here, got it? Champ slinked back to the house but stopped to lift his leg over a particularly green patch of lawn and peered back at Paul through the fence. *Don't forget, around lunchtime.*

The monster-mother stood squinting at the fence. Paul backed away slowly before turning and running back to his own house.

Paul was wrong about the salami. All they had was bologna and some crusty-looking liverwurst. He stuck a few slices of bologna in the pocket of his pajamas in case he encountered any resistance once his parents were up. Next, he hunted around for cigarettes.

His father smoked, but he didn't know what brand would suit his new half-dog. After scrounging through every side table in the house, Paul found a stubby cigar and a box of long matches, both of which he stuffed into his bologna pocket.

"What are you doing there, Ace?" Paul's dad asked, his thin hair still rumpled from the pillow. Paul knew from long experience at getting caught that you never told on yourself. Always keep mum.

"Looking to see if we have any multigrade gear oil, dad. I cut my arm on a nail and the whole thing is rusted through now." He held his father's gaze and raised his rusted arm as evidence. His dad took a knee and examined the arm, turning it over under the lamp and whistling softly when he saw the extent of the corrosion.

"Boy, that's a pretty tough one, Tiger. You know I keep the oils on the shelf in the garage, though. I'd sure hate to think you were filching one of my Palmero Gran Reservo Robusto cigars. That wouldn't be a swell thing to do, Sport."

"I won't be smoking any cigars, ever, Dad. They smell like shit." His dad nodded gravely, and they went to the garage to see what sort of oil could be applied to his arm.

"It's probably too late to undo the damage, but I think if we use axle grease, we can arrest the corrosion and prevent any further spread," his dad said. He searched the oil shelf. "This'll do it, Bubba."

Paul's father made a big show of pumping the grease gun and rubbing Paul's arm in small circles. Paul wasn't convinced anything came out of the nozzle in the first place. The whole operation was questionable, but his father made a grand show of re-inspection.

"I think we've got it wrapped up, kiddo. How about you go play in the backyard and let's not interrupt your mom's morning vodka time. How's that sound, Bear?" Paul nodded and his father patted his back.

By the time he heard the dog in the yard, the warm bologna in his pocket was stuck to the stubby little cigar.

You get the bourbon, kid? the dog asked. *What about cigarettes? And the salami?*

"I got a little cigar and some bologna. The bologna's warm now," Paul said as he pressed his eye to the knothole. The dog tilted his head and wagged his tail.

Bologna's good, throw it over. Cigar, too, come on, he said. Paul wrapped the cigar in the bologna to keep his workload down and tossed it over the fence. Instead of eating the bologna or smoking the cigar, the dog scampered back and forth on the fence line, barking and growling.

"Why are you barking?" Paul asked. "Come on, hush!" The cacophony of snarls and barking would surely interrupt his mother's morning vodka. The backdoor on the big house opened and monster-mother stepped onto the patio again. Champ galloped up to her, barking and wagging his tail and zipped back to the bologna-wrapped cigar to show her where it was.

"Traitor!" Paul yelled, but when he peeked through the knothole again, all he could see were sharp, black-stained teeth as the dog's owner— its *whole* owner—snapped at him and started climbing over the fence.

You better run, sucker! Oh, and thanks for the Palmero Gran Reservo Robusto, the dog called. Paul hightailed it back to his house, but his rusted-through arm broke off somewhere in the scramble. He peeked between the curtains and his heart skipped a beat at the sight of the woman climbing over the fence and flapping her great and terrible wings. She turned and waved at Paul with his own hand. Her jaws opened wide and she chewed and crunched his arm, hand-end first, as she dropped out of sight.

Serves me right for peeking through the fence, he thought. *But that dog is still half-mine.*

The Obvious Thing

Ingrid tore at the seatbelt. She couldn't stand to be in the car with Courtney another fucking second. She wouldn't sit there for another patronizing explanation. The seatbelt alarm chimed, and she'd gotten the door open before Courtney even noticed.

Ingrid's shoe scraped along the asphalt. If Courtney hadn't stopped, she'd have jumped.

"What are you doing?" Courtney laughed her rabid-donkey bray she used when something wasn't really funny. She scoffed, like she couldn't believe Ingrid's reaction. Cars behind them honked. Ingrid was out of the car now; her face all twisted up.

"I'm going to go give him—" Ingrid turned to the honking car. "Go around!"

The guy driving it rolled down his window. He leaned his head out of the window so his wide bovine lips and baleful eyes are visible. Like so many other men, his stigmata labeled him. Everyone could see what a bastard he's been now. Only the worst looked like cows.

"Fuck you!" His tires squealed as he swung around their argument. Everyone nearby was impressed.

"I'm just going to walk from here. That'll be the least I can do for myself, right? Just go," Ingrid said, unsatisfied with her exit line. She wanted to slam the door. She wanted to yell. She ended up embarrassed; her anger fizzled as quickly as it flared. She stood in the street in the August sun, and although she would have broken a sweat before The Change, now her scaled skin filtered the sunlight directly to her blood. Her blood was already up, though, and it boiled, almost literally. Her forehead and back prickled with delicious heat. She took three quick steps to the sidewalk and headed back to the intersection, back to the cause of this whole scene.

He was still where she'd first spotted him, shoulders slumped and watching the cars turn onto the street with his dull goat eyes. He held the cardboard sign loosely in one hand at his side. He wore shorts, but also a coat, despite the heat and the coarse hair on his legs. His hooves were crusted yellow and peeling. The Change was worse for the unhoused and most of them didn't know how to care for their new physiology.

Ingrid approached him, the crumpled bill tight in her hand. She faced him and cleared her throat. She smoothed out the money, held it out to him. "Here, I want you to have this," she said. Her voice shivered with frustration, and she realized too late that the homeless goat-man might think it was because of him.

He turned his vertical pupils to her, and then the money. "That's a lot." His pocket jingled a tune, but he kept his eyes on the money. His pocket rang again, louder this time. He accepted Ingrid's money and pulled his phone out of his pocket. He swiped a grubby finger across the screen and the jingling stopped. He returned his attention to Ingrid. He stuffed the twenty into an already bulging pocket.

"That's very kind," he said. It took Ingrid a moment to figure out he was waiting on her to leave so he could take his phone call. He stared to the horizon and scratched at his beard. For a moment, a wriggling, pale louse was visible, then burrowed out of sight again. "I'll call you back, I'm still at work."

The man hung up on his caller without saying goodbye.

Ingrid didn't know what else to say. She stalked back up the sidewalk. The goat-man had already resumed holding his sign up to oncoming traffic. The light changed and he gripped his sign with both hands. He hunched his shoulders and paced between cars. He cut a poignant figure; contrite, humble, and definitely non-threatening. It was that look that had caught Ingrid off-guard, and Courtney's callousness that set her off.

"Jeez, look at this guy," Courtney said. "Look at his sign! 'Need help, Godbless'. I'm pretty sure that's not one word." Courtney turned to Ingrid, ready to laugh.

Ingrid's lips compressed in a tight, angry white slash against her pale green scales. "He can't help it." She got out her wallet, pulled out a bill. "Give this to him."

"What? Are you serious? Most of those guys are junkies and hustlers," Courtney said. "He's probably not even homeless."

"How could you know? You can tell just by looking at him?" Ingrid spoke in sharp, clipped syllables and hissing despite her best effort not to, still holding the money out.

"I mean, yeah, honestly," Courtney said. "Most of these guys are just out here working. How many people come through here in an hour? Probably like a thousand? Maybe more? So, if even five percent of the cars going by give him a couple bucks, he probably makes, what, like a hundred dollars an hour?" She brayed and her mane bristled. "I just imagined the guy counting his money out on the counter at the bank, making a deposit."

"I don't think addiction is funny," Ingrid said.

"He's probably got a ride who picks him up. Or he calls an Uber," Courtney said. "He probably tips like a twenty."

"Lots of people are addicts. It's not a choice," Ingrid said. She hissed every word and didn't care. "It's a disease."

"I bet he takes off his coat in the car and turns up the air. He probably has his car parked around the corner. I bet it's a BMW," Courtney said. The light had changed and the car in front of them crept forward. She looked over at Ingrid, but she still wasn't laughing. Ingrid glared over at Courtney, her face twisted up.

"Oh, you've got it all figured out, Courtney? It's all simple and you just know everyone's story? You make all the right choices, right?" Ingrid couldn't recall any memory of when she was happy being with Courtney. Her focus honed in on all her judgmental bullshit.

"Did you see that guy's hooves, Ingrid? They were like scabbed over and full of pus, right? Definitely hoof and mouth disease," she said. Ingrid didn't say anything. Courtney pressed on. "Even if he is on something, he can probably afford it. Some people just won't do things for themselves. Honestly, teach a man to fish, you know?"

"We're being honest? Is it time for that now?" Ingrid's voice rose, nearly screaming. Every sibilant word came out in an extended hiss and Courtney still wasn't getting it. "Why is it so easy to just dismiss people like that? What if he just needs help?"

"He probably makes more than I do," Courtney said. By then, Ingrid had her seatbelt off and the car door open.

❧

Ingrid kept walking. She'd gone the wrong direction, walking farther from home, but she couldn't stand the idea of seeing Courtney's I-told-you-so face that she makes so well with her donkeyed features. Before The Change, Courtney's unique 'gift' was apparent, but all the donkey-people were the same. Always sticking their feet in their mouths.

"People just need help sometimes," she said. She didn't believe it, though. Not anymore.

Courtney followed her in the car. The hum of the engine, the cool relaxation of the air conditioning, both tempted her, but the heat of her anger and the sunshine stirred Ingrid's blood to walk faster.

"Ingrid, come on, what are you even doing?" Courtney asked. Ingrid ignored her.

Courtney slowed to pace Ingrid, but Ingrid refused to look over and stomped along. Her tongue flicked out, tasting the air. One of the cars nearby had passengers, tasty little mouse-children. So meek and delicious, but also hardest to catch when they started squealing and scurrying around. Ingrid stuffed down her desire to squeeze and bite, but she couldn't shake it. The desire to constrict and break and unhinge her jaw stirred her anger to new heights. If she didn't get out of the sun, her snake-brain would take over again and she'd hunt down all the delectable mouse children, and almost certainly have to pay another fine.

"Ingrid, come on, what are you even doing?" Courtney asked again. The plaintive note in her voice let Ingrid know she knows. Courtney has now realized she said all sorts of stupid things and had completely forgotten Ingrid's experience with her father. Ingrid smirked to herself and stomped down the sidewalk, trying not to entertain the memory of sucking marrow from tender bones.

Courtney parked at a McDonalds half a block ahead. She got out, made sure the truck was locked, and clopped back up the block. Ingrid remembered their first date and smiled a little, despite herself.

They'd been in the same figure study course before The Change. Courtney's critiques had been brutal, but accurate. Ingrid was angry at first, but it dissipated under the daylight of truth; she was not a talented portrait artist. She'd thought Courtney was crass, but cute. Cute as hell, actually.

"You made the model look like my grandmother, except naked," Courtney'd said.

Ingrid had laughed and knew right then that she and Courtney would see more of each other. That was the first time she'd laughed in months. Her dad was using again and no one knew where he was. The voices had started up again and he'd slipped. The needle kept the other urges at bay, he said, but the spiral made everything so much worse for everyone who loved him.

"Do you like fast food?" Courtney asked later, after class.

"Are you going to take me to McDonald's on our first date?" Ingrid's attempt to sound appalled failed.

Courtney grinned, never at a loss for words. "No, I'm just trying to get to know you at a discount," she'd said. "Taco Bell is better, and cheaper."

They'd split a combo and shared their first kiss on the playground. There were no kids around, so they didn't end up on Fox News or anything. Ingrid had imagined an outraged blond woman over a blazing graphic: *Lesbians traumatize orphans at Taco Bell!*

After The Change, when all their inward anxieties and secrets became public, they'd stayed together. It surprised them both. Courtney really had had all her stuff in a U-Haul already since her lease was up and it was cheaper than a storage unit. They'd moved in together after only a couple months, and since they were still unpacking each other's baggage when The Change came, it wasn't a deal breaker to get it all out in the open. Not many relationships survived The Change, and theirs wasn't without its problems. Their first argument was just as surreal as the changes that swept up everyone in the bizarre tide of transmogrification. In the middle of laundry day, Ingrid found out Courtney watched ahead on Bridgerton.

"I didn't think you liked it!" Courtney's mane bristled, a sign Ingrid would forever associate with equivocation.

"That shouldn't matter, Courtney, we were doing it together," Ingrid said. Courtney couldn't shout over her cold calm. Her reptilian blood moved sluggishly and despite the betrayal of trust at the core of the argument, Ingrid moved languidly and whispered her hissing recriminations.

"I'm sorry, Ingrid, I didn't realize I needed your permission." Courtney crossed her arms and stomped a hoof with a thud, despite the carpeting.

"Oh, you don't need my permission, it just shows you didn't consider me." Ingrid flicked her tongue and tasted Courtney's shame. She hadn't told anyone about the new things she could taste on the air, or how pleasurable squeezing could be.

"I'm inconsiderate again? Can't you just let it go?" The heat was building now. "That was months ago, and it didn't mean anything!"

"No, Courtney, it means you say you care, but then show me you don't," Ingrid said. The urge to bite built slowly, but Ingrid clamped it down.

"I only watched one episode, Ingrid! We can watch it again."

"I didn't watch it with you the first time! You'll do that thing you do, and you'll ruin it. You always try to talk along with the show, and then when you fuck it up, you'll spend the whole rest of the episode looking at your phone." The flavors of guilt and self-loathing floated over the static-smell of dryer sheets and detergent. Ingrid flicked her tongue again and imagined biting through fingers at each knuckle joint. Pudgy, delicious sausage fingers.

"I don't even like her anymore, Ingrid. I swear," Courtney said and hid behind folding towels. "It was a one-time thing. A mistake. That's not even fair bringing Steph up now."

"I could do other things, too, but I like spending time with you. I don't watch ahead, or text with people when we're together," Ingrid said. "You really want to talk about fair? What *is* fair, Courtney?"

"It's been over for so long. We broke up before I ever met you. And I won't say anything through the whole episode, I swear," Courtney said. "I didn't even watch the whole thing. I don't even remember what happened."

"Then you won't want to watch the next episode. And good! She's got bad breath!" Ingrid's sense-memory catalogued every flavor smell now, and Steph's breath was a mix of bacterial waste and rotting cardboard. "Look, I really don't care that you kissed Steph. I had to pull over before we'd made it two blocks and you still threw up in the car. I'm surprised you even remember it. And she tried to kiss me, like, dozens of times. But you shouldn't have watched the first episode of season two without me."

"I'm really sorry, Ingrid."

Courtney met Ingrid on the sidewalk. Ingrid didn't stop, so she fell into step alongside her. They were both hot and uncomfortable.

Courtney waited and clomped along, and Ingrid eventually spoke. "I think his pocket was full of cash. Like, a lot of money."

"I wasn't thinking about your dad," Courtney said.

"Did you see him get out his phone? It was the new iPhone," Ingrid said.

"He was wearing his coat because it would probably get it stolen if he left it somewhere," Courtney said. "It's too hot for walking right now. For me."

"You don't have to think about my dad every time we see a homeless person, Courtney. Or someone who says they are."

"Do you think he makes more than me? Like in an hour? I could probably make a sign," Courtney said. "Will put foot in mouth for money? Something like that?"

Ingrid laughed. Courtney laughed. They linked hands and kept strolling in the wrong direction.

"Where are we going?" she asked.

"I didn't think that far, I was just going to walk until you got tired of it," she said.

"Your hand is all hot and sweaty," she said.

"Well, it is the middle of August."

"I don't sweat anymore, I just vent heat," she said. "But you're making it worse by pointing it out."

"I always know exactly what to say," she said. "Usually exactly wrong."

"It's pretty obvious I know how to say the wrong thing," she said. "I'm good at the obvious thing."

"Do you want to get Taco Bell?" she asked.

Fists in the Night

We prowled the night, thirsting for righteous justice the way a starving cat sizes up a cornered rat. My brother Brian and I appeared to be just two regular, non-karate assholes, but when we slip on our *gis* and cinch our yellow belts, we're the Fists in the Night. This is an exclusive club, though we're working on a membership form. No regular assholes allowed.

"Ok, let's do our kata again, Brian," I said and assumed my ready stance.

"Bleeyargh!" Brian launched himself across the alley, completely ignoring the first two moves. He's supposed to high block and then do a side kick, but he skipped right to the lunging dick punch and tripped over a garbage can in the dark. Plus his headband kept slipping down and he couldn't see too good.

"Quit messing around, goofwad!" I kicked him right in his taint for making a ruckus, and he retaliated with a frog punch to my neck. I was ready to kick his ass in earnest when a wolf whistle echoed from across the street. It was Kenny Wiggins and his stupid friend Billy Williams. I'd been practicing my kata for three weeks; I was ready for a fight. "What kind of parents name their kid William Williams? Dumbasses, that's what kind! And why don't you ass-shaped lamewads get a life?"

"You guys look like fucking dorks in your pajamas!" Kenny yelled back.

He doesn't know anything about karate, or he'd know this yellow belt means I'll axe-kick him right in his stupid collarbone. We got in a fight last year. We'd only gotten as far as pushing each other before the whole thing got broken up by Mrs. Allen. After four or five more pushes, I definitely would have punched him. That's why I started taking karate, since I've never punched anyone except Brian. I explained how it was good for self-discipline and self-confidence, and maybe a few other self-centered things that I didn't mention, like looking totally badass in the karate outfit, when I pitched the idea to my parents. But Mom said I had to take Brian, too.

I flipped Kenny the bird.

"Hey! You better quit giving me the finger or I'll kick your ass again, Floberts!" Kenny's stupid face turned red, and I saluted him with the finger some more.

Brian pulled down his pants and mooned them, but his yellow belt tripped him up and he knocked over another trash can. A light came on in Mr. Brajbhoomi's apartment.

"I'll give you a crescent kick to your taint, Biggins!" I yelled, letting the middle-finger birds fly free. He charged and I got ready to high block. Nothing could get through my high block. I've practiced it like twenty times a day.

He swung at me with this weird softball-pitch-style slap attack. I didn't train to block that, so I tried to front kick him. Everyone in karate class stood still and waited for you to kick them; Kenny kept moving.

"Hold still, dickhole!" He kept skipping around to try and slap at me again. I was pretty sure that was cheating, but we didn't lay out the rules before we started fighting, so I couldn't really bring it up. But I was at my boiling point with this jerk. As soon as he held still long enough, I was going to inside crescent kick him and follow it up with a punch right to his chest. Sensei said that kind of punch can stop a grown man's heart, but I didn't care. I was sick of Kenny making fun of me and I'd risk going to jail for not registering my fists as deadly weapons.

Brian still had his pants down and kept jumping backward, ass first at Billy Williams. It was the dumbest thing I've ever seen, but Billy didn't want to get Brian's butt flakes on him, so he kept dodging away.

"Hey, you dumb-asses, cut that shit out! Shut up and go home before I call all your parents!" Mr. Brajbhoomi stood on the stoop in his boxers and undershirt, his face red from yelling.

"I kicked your ass again, Floberts!" Kenny screamed over his shoulder as he bolted down the street. Coward.

"Nuh-uh, I kicked your ass, Figgins!" I hollered back, but I don't think he heard me. I turned to Mr. Brajbhoomi and put my fist in my open hand and bowed to him like my sensei taught me. "Not to worry, Mr. Brajbhoomi! We'll be patrolling the neighborhood regularly. If you see any other idiots like Kenny Wiggins, just give us a call."

Not-my-brother Brian

Brian and I finally made it to the mall fountain, but it wasn't the same as I remembered from last summer. It was half-empty and most of the little squirty parts weren't squirting.

"Malls everywhere are dying," Dad told us last summer with a smile like it was funny, but it made me sad. I thought everyone loved the mall. There were more stores gone than open still, so I guess Dad was right. He only ever came to the mall to go to stupid Radio Shack anyway. That store sucked so much.

"We should wish for a million dollars!" Brian jumped up and down like he had to pee.

"No, it's my quarter and I'm going to wish for something I want, not something for a butt-finger like you." I gripped the quarter in my sweaty fist safe in my pocket.

"No, it's Mom's quarter and she said you had to share it with me. You're the butt-finger, you dirty butt-finger smeller!"

I checked to see if Mom could see from Hair Safari, and I didn't think she could. I punched Brian in the arm and gave him a tit-ty-twister. This twerp was always bringing up this thing Mom said one time, or telling me 'that's against the law!' and I was sick of it.

"Ow, you piece of crap!" He yelled loud enough for his whininess to echo in the mostly empty mall. I was about to punch him again when he wrapped himself around my leg like we did to Dad before he said we were too big to walk us around the house. And then the little bastard bit me.

"Get off me, you unitard!" I slapped at his head, without thinking, and the quarter slipped from my hand. It flashed in the lights over the fountain, even though about half of them were burned out.

"I wish you weren't my brother!" Brian yelled and rubbed the side of his head where I'd gotten him with a good slap. The quarter landed in the fountain with a plop. A shower of sparks burst out of the lights, and a strange snapping sensation washed over me, like some invisible thread had been cut. At that moment, I got the sense that each of us in this life are connected by invisible strands of love, tying us together and binding our fates on some greater cosmic scale, or something equally dumb.

I gaped, turning over the fact I didn't have a brother anymore in my mind. The last time I didn't have a brother, I was three, and I barely remembered any of it. All the memories of him touching my baseball cards, riding my bike, and generally being a pain in my ass faded away. They were like a dream, the way I'd try to hold onto when when I woke up, but they'd just slip right away no matter how hard I concentrated. And then it dawned on me what he'd done.

"You wasted my wish! I'm gonna tell everyone at school you love The Oak Ridge Boys!" I tried to elbow-drop the little dork, not-my-brother Brian, but the coward curled up into a ball and started screeching. "I'm glad you're not my brother anymore, I'm gonna pound the crap out of you!"

Just as I'd managed to pin his arm down and get a few good frog punches in, a cold hand closed around my arm, above my elbow. Mom said her hands stayed cold since she started working on the chicken salad packing line. I thought chickens ate bugs, but maybe they're special vegetarian chickens at Mom's job.

"If you two little shits don't cut it out, I'll bang your heads together. Quit rolling around on the floor like a couple of dingleberries and behave! Brian, I'll let your parents know what a little dork you are, too." Mom had aluminum foil all over her head and she hiss-yelled at me in her embarrassing-me-in-public voice around a cigarette. "I'm not carting you and your friend around for you to act like heathens, Jake." She lifted us both up off the floor, dropped us on our butts, and marched back to Hair Safari.

"You're the dingleberry, shit-breath," I told not-my-brother Brian and landed another frog punch on his arm because I was sure my mom wasn't looking.

"Ow! I told you my mom doesn't want us hanging out because I always come home with bruises! Quit punching me, dickbreath." Brian kicked me in the shin and scampered away, laughing.

I would tell everyone at school he loved The Oak Ridge Boys. I didn't even know why we were friends.

The Devastation of the space-Viking

I spent my whole childhood terrified of the space-Viking. My grandpa warned me about the hordes of blonde-haired, grey-headed invaders at least once a week, but he always whispered so my mom and dad couldn't hear.

"If you don't learn algebra, the space-Viking will kick you in the balls while you're takin' a bath. It's impossible to defend yourself in the bathtub, Jake. Learn math." Anytime Grandpa said words with S in them, his teeth whistled. And his breath always carried the same smell asphalt makes when it rains in the summertime.

I spent every bathtime after that watching the door, ready to fling a shampoo bottle at the first weirdo in a horned helmet who stormed through it. I aced all my math tests, but I stayed on high alert anyway.

"The space-Viking is crafty, Jake. He wears disguises, did I ever tell you that?" Grandpa has a weird tooth, just off to the side of the front ones. I see it back there when he smiles, brown like a potato. "Did you ever get a good look at Mrs. McLarty down the library three weeks ago? Was she right-handed, or left-handed the last time you were in there? She might be him, just in disguise, and he's getting away with it because you didn't look close enough."

I kept a list of the things Grandpa told me about space-Vikings, and I recognized the immediate danger my own carelessness placed me in. I vowed to pay attention to the small details, starting with who did what with which hand. I couldn't remember if Mrs. McLarty signed my books out with her right or left hand. I vowed to keep a list of which hand people used. Vigilance was clearly key to keep from getting kicked in the balls.

Grandpa used his left hand to pick the strings on the guitar, that's why it's strung upside down.

Mom peeled potatoes with her right hand.

Dad signed the checkbook with his right hand.

My best friend Jonesy threw with his right hand. He tried throwing a rock with his left hand when I told him about my list. He sucked at throwing with either hand we discovered, but I'd know if Jonesy were the space-Viking anyway.

"Are you sure the space-Viking is even a real thing? My Grandpa took me snipe hunting one time, but it was bullshit. There's no such thing as snipes, and even if there were, they wouldn't live in the woods behind Walgreens." Jonesy tried throwing another rock with his right hand, but he let go early and it bounced off his ear. The rock left a cut in the exact shape of a cucumber.

"We should probably keep an eye out to be safe. But don't tell too many people I've got this list. We don't want to tip off the space-Viking, just in case he's real." I tried throwing a rock with my right hand and I pegged it right in the middle of the handicap parking sign. "Grandpa says he has a big round gray head and blonde braids, but he can wear disguises."

"Sounds like a really ugly woman." Jonesy squinted at the sign. "Try with your left."

I threw another rock and pegged it again.

The next day at school, Jonesy told Kevin Leeward, Jason Feldman, and Billy Williams that I could throw with both hands. But he told Billy about the list and that pissed me off a little. Out of all the kids we were friends with at school, Billy Williams was lowest on the friendship scale. He always had his mouth open, and he moved his finger down the page and whispered the words whenever he read anything.

"Jonesy told me about your list, Jake. Put down that I'm right-handed at golf." He shoved his hands in his pockets and stood there with his mouth open and his shoulders hunched up, like his neck had disappeared.

"Golf? Why would golf ever come up, Billy? You think if the space-Viking comes along one day, we'll figure out his secret on the golf course? You're gonna get kicked in the balls a lot, Billy."

"Put it down as mini golf, then. And make me left-handed at mini golf." He pretended to putt an invisible ball with an invisible putter, but he was doing it right-handed.

"Which is it, Billy? Are you right-handed or left-handed at mini golf?"

He shrugged and held his hands up with a stupid smile on his face. "How can you tell?"

"The list is just something I made up when Jonesy and I were throwing rocks, that's all. It's not really a thing I'm doing." I had the list folded up in my back pocket.

Mr. Jim, the janitor, scraped gum off the bottom of the lunch table with his right hand.

Miles Drury used both hands to hang the flag on the rope on the flagpole this morning before school, but I've seen his jump-shot in basketball and he's right-handed.

"Put down that Susan Miller is left-handed." Billy wasn't giving up. I ignored him while I counted to thirty in my head, but he didn't go away.

"Is she?" I'd never seen Susan do anything now that I thought about it.

"Is she what?" Billy breathed through his mouth.

"Left-handed."

Billy shrugged and held his hands up again with the same smile as before. "How can you tell?"

I practiced more throws with baseballs, footballs, and tennis balls while Billy pretended to keep putting. I threw just as well with either hand, not like Jonesy. I hit what I was aiming for every time. I wanted Billy to go away, but he kept giving me names for the list.

Jonesy went home early from school because the cucumber-shaped cut he got on his ear from the rock got infected. It turned angry red and swelled up. I hoped it would turn green and stay that way, like a tattoo. It would serve him right for leaving me stuck with Billy following me around and running his mouth all day.

"Principal Chalmers is right-handed. I saw him picking his nose with his right hand."

"Billy, the list is supposed to be secret, ok? You can't tell anyone about it, otherwise the space-Viking will know we're onto him and I don't want to get my balls devastated." My dad told me that getting kicked in the balls is devastating. He made it sound like you'd probably have to move to a different town, or get a new job, with that kind of injury.

"I'm not going to tell anyone else except Kenny." Billy was the only kid who liked Kenny Wiggins.

"Which hand does Kenny touch your butt with, Billy?"

"Kenny's left-handed." Billy punched me on the arm with his right hand.

I went to the library after school to see if I could learn anything else about the space-Viking and I carefully studied Mrs. McLarty's desk out of the corner of my eye when I walked by. I didn't want to be close to discovering the space-Viking's secret identity only to get kicked in the balls at the last minute. I didn't see her writing anything, but I did notice she had a smear of blue ink on her left pinky, so when I got to a desk, I added her to the list. Mrs. McLarty, left-handed librarian. After that, I searched the card catalogs for whatever they had on the space-Viking, but all I found was *Vikings, Minnesota* and a bunch of books about medieval raiders who could cross the ocean in their longboats. They didn't kick people in the balls, though, mainly they sacked and pillaged and then sailed back home. I finally decided to ask Mrs. McLarty if the library had any old articles on microfilm, but she squinted from behind her cat-eyes glasses and shook her head.

"There's no such thing as a space-Viking," she said, but her mouth twitched when she said it. I studied her for signs of disguise, but I couldn't be sure. Her hair was maybe a little blonder than the last time, but it looked more like a pile of spaghetti noodles balanced on top of her head than braids. Still, I backed away from her desk without turning around, just in case.

When I got home that day, I told my mom and dad about being able to throw with either hand.

"What do you think it means, Dad? I can throw pretty much any kind of ball with either hand." I pulled a tennis ball out of my pocket. "You want to see?"

"Sure thing, Jake, let me just finish up here," Dad said and bent over his checkbook. He always ordered plain blue checks with his name and address in the top corner, but not my mom's.

"Why isn't Mom's name on the checks?" I'd never thought to ask before.

"Because we have separate checking accounts, Jake. We have different tastes in checks, so we decided to just open separate accounts. It stopped all the fights dead in their tracks."

My dad had a big black leather folio he keeps his checks in and it always smelled like maple syrup. I never remembered to ask why when he had it out. "What kind of checks does Mom like?"

"Clowns." Dad snapped his folio shut and put it in its cupboard over the kitchen desk. "Show me these throws, Jake."

We went in the backyard and I threw the tennis ball five times with my right hand, and then five times with my left.

"I didn't know you were ambidextrous Jake, what a talent!" Dad kept lobbing the ball back to me like he thought I couldn't take a hard throw.

"Come on, Dad, put some heat on it!" I whooped and threw the ball to him as hard as I could. He caught it wide-eyed and grinned at me. The tennis ball had *curved* in mid-air when I threw it. He threw a winger back to me and I caught it one-handed.

"Oh, hey, that's a good catch, Jakey-boy!" Grandpa had wandered downstairs and watched us with his hands on his hips.

"I can throw with both hands, Grandpa!" I tossed him the tennis ball and he threw it back with his right hand.

"Is that right? Show me a throw with your left." I did and Grandpa whistled and threw it back right-handed again.

I tossed him another one, dead-on, and this time he clapped. Dad clapped, too. They both walked over to the middle of the yard and patted me on the back.

"That's really great, Jake. What a talent!" Dad clapped me on the back again.

"Yeah, that's marvelous, Jake, but say, do you remember what I told you a while back about disguises?" Grandpa smiled, but his crusty brown tooth wasn't there. It clicked into place then, but I was too late.

Before I could answer, or guard my balls, Grandpa's whole body shimmered and there he was, the space-Viking, with his bulbous, gray head, long braids, and blonde beard. He kicked me right in the balls and teleported away in a shower of sparks before Dad could grab him. I rolled around on the grass, my devastated balls aching with that gonna-throw-up, sinking pain. It was so much worse than what Dad had said. I was probably going to have to change schools, or go live in the woods like a hermit. I groaned, but I could only take shallow breaths. When I flopped over to face the other direction, Grandpa limped into the yard wearing his bathrobe, hunched over at the waist.

"Hey! Did you two get a good look at him? Damn space-Viking kicked me right in the balls while I was in the bathtub!"

Garbage Juice

There was so much garbage buried everywhere now that if you dug a hole, it filled with garbage juice that smelled like sour vomit and moldy coffee. Even though plastic wasn't biodegradable, chemicals still leached out of it, causing some kind of underground catastrophe. Scientists complained about it on TV a lot, but I never paid any attention. It was just how things were. My husband Doug knew better, of course, and dug a hole anyway. Now the back yard smells like shit and I really don't believe he knows how to build a fence since the sum of his knowledge came from watching one video.

"That smells like shit! Why'd you dig a hole?" I've asked questions with obvious answers all my life.

"How are we supposed to replace our fence without digging holes?" Doug worried about the dogs getting out, so he knocked down a whole section of fence. I really don't think that was necessary, but he's full of the special kind of indignance he gets when the world isn't how it *should* be. Now we've got a pile of lumber, a shovel, and some bags of concrete.

"Can't we just nail boards up?" I waited there with my hands on my hips. He kept going on about it until my phone rang. Milwaukee area code. "Hello?"

"Irma Douglas?" I didn't recognize the nasal, northern-accented voice. "Is this Irma Douglas? This is Verlinda from Emery Grove."

Nothing registered for a moment, but then the needle clicked into the groove. Emery Grove. Milwaukee. Mom. "This is Irma, yes. Is this about my mother? Is she ok?"

"This call may be being recorded for quality and training purpose. I'm calling to let you know that Elaine Murph's account is delinquent." The woman paused.

"What do you mean? We're making payments, Janet and I. And what about the long-term care insurance?" I stepped away from Doug and his garbage-juice hole. My stomach twisted up and my mouth watered. I took a calming breath. This was a misunderstanding.

"No, ma'am, the payments we're receiving from you aren't enough to cover the outstanding balances and your mother's long term care policy not issuing payments. That company has went bankrupt and we're not currently receiving payment from your sister Janet." Her grammar grated my nerves, but I kept my voice even.

"How far behind are we, exactly? And did you say they went bankrupt? And wait— Janet's *not* making payments?"

"That is correct, yes. They has went bankrupt and Elaine Murph's account is in arrears for the last four months. This matter has been turned over to collections and we're proceeding with eviction proceedings at the end of the current billing cycle if we don't receive our payment in full." I hated her immediately, this woman calling from Milwaukee demanding money, making threats, and butchering spoken English.

"What do you mean? You're just going to kick her out? She has Alzheimer's! And have you called my sister Janet? Did you talk to her about her half of the payments?" Cold sweat pricked my armpits, my back. My heart turned a slow somersault.

"We has been hoping to engage in discussions with Ms. Chalmers about her financial obligations, but we're unable to reach her, phone-wise." The longer she talked, the more this woman reminded me of a grackle squawking from a tree. Like she knew she was safe and got to shit on everyone.

"What are you saying, I'm sorry? Have you talked to Janet or not? How much are we short?" The dogs barked behind me. Doug shouted amid a clatter of wood. He'd dropped the post he was attempting to set.

"What the fuck! Hey! This is my property, what are you doing?" Doug took a step backward and tripped over his concrete bags, landing hard on his ass. He sat there yelling at a stranger climbing up out of the hole he'd dug.

"I'm sorry, I'm going to have to call you back!" I hung up and hurried over to the dogs. "Jan! Scout! Inside! Now!"

The dogs were both chickenshit; they trotted back to the house, barking over their shoulders the whole way. Doug scrambled to his feet and grabbed up his shovel. The stranger's head and one arm stuck out of the hole. He didn't have a face, or skin as far as I could tell, and his arm swam around for something to grab onto. Wet, slime-dripping fingers grasped, digging into the soil, and he pulled himself out of the hole.

"Hey! Quit trying to climb out of that hole!" Doug brandished the shovel like he was going to bash the stranger emerging from the garbage juice.

"Doug, quit! What are you going to do, hit him with the shovel?" I put a hand on his shoulder, but he shrugged me off.

"Self-defense, Irma! This is our property!" Doug stabbed the guy's head and the shovel squelched. Direct hit. A smell like rotten eggs and spoiled meat hissed out of his wound.

I gagged and my eyes watered. "Oh, God, that's so bad! Why'd you do that?"

Doug trotted a few steps, dropped the shovel, and puked in the grass. The dogs barked through the window, safe inside the house. The stranger pulled more of himself out of the hole, but he only had one arm. He knelt on the grass and reached back into the murky liquid to pull out another arm. The wound on his head oozed black goop, but he didn't seem bothered. Hard to tell with no face, though.

"Um, hello? Garbage sir? Why did you come out of that hole?" I backed away as I asked. The smell floated between us. He turned his head toward me while he squished his arm into place, but didn't speak. No mouth. "Maybe you could go back?"

"Kick him, Irma! Make him get back in the hole! This is our yard!" Doug wiped his mouth with the back of his hand, but he wasn't done throwing up.

"I'm not kicking him, Doug!" While we yelled, the garbage man stood up and stretched his arms and legs. He turned his empty face toward me again and tilted his head the same way Jan the Dog did when I talked to her. He bent down and reached into the hole. He pulled fistfuls of mud and detritus out and slapped them onto his face. When he looked at me again, he had eyes, a nose, and a mouth. The placement was off, like he only knew approximately where they should be, so his expression was decidedly lopsided. His face glistened with fresh garbage juice, too. "This...your...yard?"

"Um...yes, this is our yard. Can I get you a towel, maybe, if you're going back where you came from?" I hoped he'd say no. I wanted to be polite, but without going near him. Maybe I could throw a roll of paper towels at him, basketball-style, from the back porch.

"I go now, need job. Eat plastic. Hungry. Goodbye, miss." The garbage guy stepped through the hole in the fence and wandered away, peering this way and that as he walked up the sidewalk. I supposed it was the first time he'd been above ground, so everything must look new.

"Why didn't you kick him, Irm—" Doug held up a finger and threw up again.

⁂

"What? Why didn't you call them back?" I tried not to lose my temper, but Janet made it hard.

"I didn't recognize the number, Irma! I don't answer the phone when I don't recognize it. But they sent something in the mail about four months ago, yeah." Janet yawned, like she was bored with this conversation already.

"Janet! Why didn't you call me four months ago? This is serious! They're going to evict our mother!"

"I thought they sent you one too, I guess. And they can't evict her, can they? Isn't that illegal?" She crunched something in my ear—Janet was partial to cheese puffs.

"No, they can totally evict her. Why aren't you making your half of the payments? They have dozens of ways th—wait, when was the last time you went to see her?" I tried counting to ten in my mind. And then I tried counting to one hundred.

"When was the last time? Uh, probably Easter? Oh, did you see the thing about the garbage people? They gave one a job at Sheboygan's washing dishes. He gets paid in garbage. Did you know they all eat garbage? Like, for food?" I swear I heard her filing her nails, too.

"You haven't been to see Mom in almost six months!" I counted to two hundred while my vision blurred.

"So? You haven't been since Christmas! Don't yell at me!"

"Janet," I said and took a deep, calming breath, "we live in Orlando. Emery Grove is a five-minute drive from your house. You have to go up there tomorrow and see if we can straighten this out. I will help however I can, but I need you to step up here. Why haven't you been making the payments?"

Janet didn't say anything, but a plastic bag crinkled over the phone.

"Irma, Jesus, I'll go by there when I have time! I have to work, too, you know? Mom doesn't know the difference anyway. Bye!" Janet crunched in my ear one more time before she hung up. I slammed my phone down on the counter. The screen was already cracked. Doug yelled from the couch.

"Hey, can you believe this shit? They're all over the country!" He held up his phone and pointed at it like I could read it from the next room.

"Are you talking about the garbage people? Janet told me one got a job at Sheboygan's washing dishes."

"They get paid in garbage, Irma! How's that even fair?" Doug scrolled manically, eyes bugging out of his face.

"I know, right? Shouldn't they get paid with money? Garbage is kind of everywhere, isn't it? Like for free?" I must have missed something, because Doug gave me a look like I'd just said *panties*. He's always hated that word.

"No, it's not fair they're taking people's jobs. They're going to work places and taking jobs from real people! I just read a thing that said they're starting them out in Public Works right here in town! Roadkill technicians." I recognized Doug's strident outrage was only getting started, but I couldn't help myself.

"Do you want that job, El? And didn't you complain for two weeks about the dead raccoon around the corner from your office?"

"That's not the point, Irma! These guys work for garbage! It's not fair. You watch, they'll be everywhere in no time. We never should have let them climb out of the ground." He kept scrolling. He didn't even look up or ask what I'd been talking to Janet about. "Jesus, Jolly George's is going to have them collect grocery buggies from the parking lot! The buggies will be filthy!"

"My mom's going to get kicked out of her memory care unit. I don't know what I'm going to do about it." I waited for him to look up and cross the room and hug me. I needed him to tell me it would work out. We'd be ok.

"I mean, seriously, who wants to use a cart with garbage juice all over it?" He scoffed and scrolled some more.

I called Emery Grove again, determined to keep my cool and find out what options were available to us to keep mom living there. Someone answered on the first ring.

"Hello? You need?" The person on the other end spoke with a wet, slapping accent I didn't recognize.

"Hello? Is this Emery Grove?"

"Yes. Emery Grove. I help." It landed then; it was a garbage person working up there in Milwaukee now. Definitely an improvement.

"Hi, this is Irma Douglas. My mother, Elaine Murph, lives there. I was calling to see if we can discuss some kind of payment plan to get her account current?" There was only silence for a moment, then the garbage person spoke again.

"Call being recorded. Training purpose. I can help payment arrangement. Please hold." The line clicked and the hold music started up, the weird one that sounded like massive wires being plucked by a giant. I looked up the nursing home's website while I waited in case there was a corporate number I could call for payment plans or credit if this didn't work. I clicked things that until I was reading about the company's nationwide network of homes and plan for increased short-term profitability.

The investor relations section of the webpage listed dozens of initiatives, but the most prominent update outlined their aggressive hiring of 'ground people' and how they were really improving the bottom line while also eliminating waste disposal expenses as a bonus. They expected a record profit in the third quarter. I idly wondered where all the people who'd done the jobs before were going to work, but I was derailed by a click and a busy signal.

"What the fuck?" I dialed the number again.

"Hello? You need?" It was the same one as before.

"This is Irma Douglas, we got cut off before. I was calling to ask about a payment plan for my moth—"

"Call record being for training maybe. I can transfer to payment plan helping. Hold please." I couldn't tell how long they'd been doing the job, but they sounded more confident this time around and hung up on me immediately.

When I tried calling back again, the phone rang until the line clicked several times and a recording played. "Hello and thank you for calling Emery Glen. Our office hours are Monday through Friday from eight AM to nine forty-five AM. We appreciate your patience as we undergo some staffing changes to make your experience the best it can be! Please leave a message and we'll return your call as soon as possible."

The line clicked and a busy signal buzzed in my ear again. I started to call back again but Doug burst in, yelling, face twisted in a paroxysm of outrage.

"They laid me off! Those fuckers went and did it! They replaced the entire marketing department with fucking garbage people!" He turned toward me, and I saw he'd burst a blood vessel in his eye.

"Doug, calm down! Start at the beginning—what happened?" I kicked a chair out for him. "Oh, and I think we're supposed to call them ground people."

Instead of sitting, Doug paced back and forth and waved his arms while he yelled about the injustice he'd suffered. "Good luck trying to coordinate Evangelical-Friendly Fantasy Day and Gay Week with a bunch of garbage eaters controlling the ad spend! The park is going to go straight to shit! And have you been out, Irma? They're everywhere! The whole city is full of garbage people now!"

I dialed again and the phone rang, but I got the same message as before. I slammed my phone on the table in frustration. Doug still paced and ranted. "Doug, calm down and we'll figure it out, ok? Didn't you always say a trained monkey could work in marketing, anyway? Maybe this is the sign you needed to go get that MBA you've been talking about."

"Okra! Grabble... f-fuck! Dwecky glibble ch-ch-ch—" Doug stumbled into the table. The left side of his face sagged, and he tried to stand up again. He could only reach for the chair with one arm.

I woke up because my phone rang, but I didn't have any idea where I was. I lay stretched out over several chairs in the emergency surgery waiting room. Doug had a stroke; I remembered. My phone was still ringing, Milwaukee area code. It took several tries to swipe and answer and the broken screen nicked my finger. I really need to throw this one out and get a new one. "Hello?"

"Irma Douglas? This Verlinda Emery Grove. Training call recorded purposes." This wasn't the same Verlinda I talked to a few days ago. It was a garbage-mouthed ground person with their stupid wet voice.

"Look, I've been trying to call you and work out some kind of payment plan, ok? You keep hanging up on me!" I realized I was yelling, and I didn't care. I'd woken some of the other people in the waiting room and they stared at me owlishly.

"Elaine Murph dead. Sorry for loss. Shipping department call to move dead person. Hungry now?"

"Don't you dare eat my mother, you horrible fucking garbage person!" A dozen other things I wanted to say crashed together in my mind, but I couldn't say anything else through the tears. I needed to call Janet. I couldn't figure out what to do first and the person on the phone spoke.

"Need money, pay bill for resident. Sorry dead." The line clicked and the familiar busy signal buzzed in my ear.

I laughed. I was still laughing when a wet hand landed on my shoulder. I looked up at the same face I'd seen the garbage person smush together after crawling out of the hole in my backyard. His head still oozed goop where Doug whacked him with the shovel.

"I doctor. Husband. Him left-side paralyzed. Please billing department for invoice payment. Discharge after pay." The garbage doctor grimaced down at me and patted my shoulder, leaving it juicy, and with a faint whiff of ammonia. I started giggling. The giggles turned into laughter and then quickly snowballed into screaming peals of hilarity.

I decided I'd go home and dig a hole and climb into it.

Author's Note

'I can do better than that!' you thought, and then set out to do just that.

I think we've all had this moment and I hope you had that reaction reading at least one of these stories. Or reading them made you feel like you can write your own story, at least; maybe not everyone feels like they need to beat someone else. I decided I wanted to start writing all the way back in elementary school, so I did. It was awful, but I'd written a story about a karate expert who lived in a house devoid of televisions and furniture (except for a bed—even karate masters sleep) so he could live that total-karate lifestyle. Plenty of room for karate practice. One day his karate rival broke into his house, registered surprise at his nemesis's lack of furniture, and then even greater surprise when he discovered his sworn enemy waited for him inside.

There was an epic karate fight where neither of them could gain the upper hand, so skilled were they both at their craft.

By the end of it, both men learned, grew, and appreciated each other's strength of character. When I was a child, I believed most of life's future problems would be solved with karate. My brother Gavin, the only other living person to read my karate story, issued this review after reading it: *This is the worst story ever written.*

Even if you feel like one of these is the worst story ever written, I hope any of them made you laugh, or made you think, or made you want to write one of your own. Inspiration comes from weird places, and I usually put some of myself into each story, like Elliott's desperation for a dad to teach him very specific things in *A Machine for Hugs*. I always wanted my dad to be around, and more importantly, understand me as a person and help me figure out my place in the world, but that's not how it worked out. The father in *Weeding* is very closely based on my own real-life father, who may as well have been a space alien. Anytime we went on a car ride when we were kids, my dad would ask "Who wants McDonalds?" and, of course, we all did. "Well, point it out if you see one!"

He'd drive along, playing like he didn't see it as all four of us screamed and pointed and wet our pants over the McDonald's he was passing.

"What? There was a McDonald's? Dammit! I missed it!" he'd say. Every single time. Life is complicated and sometimes you get what you get. I sometimes wonder how my mother, some of whom the mother in *Weeding* is based on, put up with him at all.

There's quite a lot of my own childhood imaginings in *A Rusting Boy*, as I spent a lot of my time as a kid alone, despite having three siblings. I wandered through the house, backyard, and everywhere else totally absorbed in my own world, which often as not led to some kind of trouble. One time, I wandered away and got lost. I found a nice stranger's house and called home. Kids knew their home phone numbers back then...in case they got lost. I had friends, but even as a young teen, I got a sense that you could be friends with someone and also not like them very much at all. The boys in *We Were Always Bored* are somewhat based on some of those relationships.

So yeah, there's a little bit of my life, real and imagined, in each of these stories and I hope you enjoyed them. If any of them sparked a thought in you, or the desire to tell your own story, I really hope you do. Writing has been the most fulfilling hobby I've ever had and it's full of self-doubt, frustration, imposter syndrome, and myriad other insecurities. Knowing that, I bet you can't wait to get started.

The illustrations on the cover and the end of some of the stories are by my good friend Jason Tetreault. His bio states: Jason Tetreault lives and works in Bartlett, Tennessee, and spends a lot of time doodling nonsense. He is often annoyed that spicy food isn't all that spicy. His girlfriend Cara makes anything he does possible, and she's a saint for putting up with him. He's an amazing artist and an even better friend.

Thanks for reading my stories.

Galen Gower